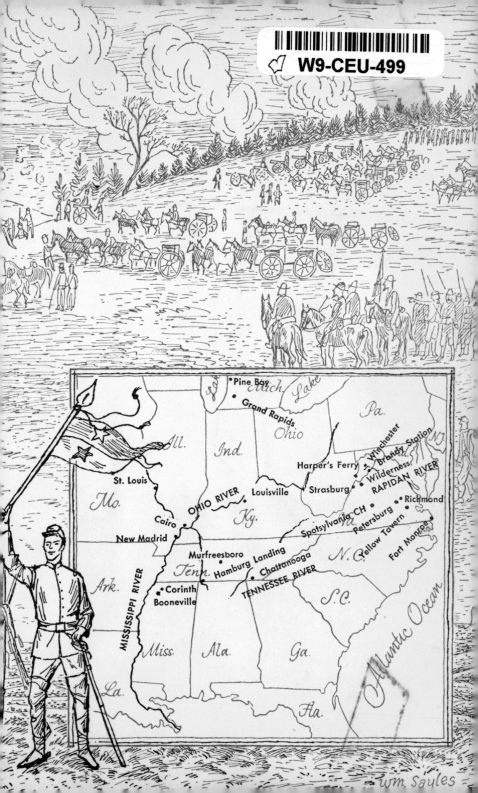

W9-CEU-499

wm. sayles

BANNERS AT SHENANDOAH

BANNERS

DOUBLEDAY & COMPANY, INC.,

Bruce Catton

AT SHENANDOAH

A Story of Sheridan's Fighting Cavalry

GARDEN CITY, NEW YORK, 1955

CAVALCADE
BOOKS

With the exception of actual historical personages identified as such, the characters are entirely the product of the author's imagination and have no relation to any person or event in real life.

LIBRARY OF CONGRESS CATALOG CARD NUMBER 55-5579

For DAVIS CATTON

CONTENTS

BANNERS AT SHENANDOAH

1. THE MAGIC GLASS

He was a wiry little man with short legs and long arms, and he used to wear a floppy felt hat jammed any which way on his black round head. He was swarthy and he had a big mustache, and when nothing much was going on he could look sleepy and sullen. People who saw him then could make the mistake of thinking he was dull and stupid.

But that was just when things were quiet. In battle it was different.

When the guns were firing and the air was full of dust and smoke and racket, and everything was going wrong, then Phil Sheridan would come rocketing up on his big black horse, looking three times larger than life, his skin darker than ever, his eyes glowing as if he had a flame in him somewhere. And no matter how tired or scared or fed up you might be, you would suddenly feel that everything was going to be all right now, and you would set out to do whatever that man told you to do even if you did figure that it couldn't possibly be done. As likely as not you would cheer your head off while you were doing it.

He had a lot of staff officers, like any other major general, but they were usually off somewhere working. When Sheridan came up he was apt to be all alone, except for a soldier riding at his heels carrying Sheridan's personal flag. That was a little red-and-white swallowtail with two stars on it, a major general's flag. You could always count on seeing it right up in the front line, where major generals didn't often bother to go, and the hotter things were up front, the more certain you could be that that flag was going to show up with the general just ahead of it.

Sometimes Sheridan would carry the flag himself. Probably he rode his horse at a walk once in a while—even that big brute Rienzi (that was his favorite horse) couldn't gallop all the time—but somehow I don't really believe it. No soldier who ever fought under him can remember him in any other way than as riding at a gallop, that little flag snapping in the wind, his hat crumpled in one fist; and when he did ride up, no matter how many other men were around you, you always got the feeling that when he went by he was looking right at you personally.

That was what did it. It was just as if he was telling you that you were really as good a man as he was if you'd just make the effort to act that way. He wasn't getting hurt so you probably wouldn't get hurt either, and even if you did why somehow if he was there it wouldn't matter much. It was foolish of you to feel that way, but that's what the sight of him did to you, and for just a minute or two—the minute or two that really counted—you would be his kind of soldier.

I have seen men who had run five miles to get out of danger turn around and hurry straight back into what they had just run away from, simply because they had seen him waving his hat and calling to them, a quarter of a mile away. Men with bullets in them, only half a minute from dying, would stumble to their feet and try to go on, because he had yelled out that they weren't really hurt. Soldiers who had been in the army long enough to know what a bloody swindle war really is would begin to feel that army life was really kind of fun, as long as Sheridan was up front.

It all happened a long time ago, to be sure. When an old soldier looks back he is apt to see things through a magic glass—a glass that filters out the pain and the mud, the evil and the hardship, and restores the golden light of the old days, so that everything looks better than it really was.

But there were things about Phil Sheridan that you don't need a magic glass to see. He had victory in him: not just victory over the enemy on the battlefield, but victory over whatever it is men have to fight against inside themselves.

It's as if he would be telling you: You can't help being scared but you don't need to let fear take charge because you can be stronger than fear if you want to; anyway, maybe your fear is nothing but the Old Nick himself making your heart quake and telling you to look out for your own precious skin when that isn't what really matters at all, so come on and we'll dispose of him together, once and for all and forever. . . .

When you fought for him he could say all of that to you without speaking a word. Maybe it was the way he tilted his black bullet head, or the way he would shake that little flag over the battle smoke, or the way he would get between you and danger and then ride silhouetted against the wild red glare of what you were afraid of. Whatever the trick was, he could do it, and he could make you respond to it, and you would remember it all the rest of your life.

Besides that, he was just about the last of the world's great cavalry commanders. He could make war seem exciting and colorful even to men who had been in many battles, and somehow nobody has quite been able to do it that way since. He struck hard and he left terrible scars, and most people either loved him a great deal or hated him with a bitter hatred, for there never was any middle ground about him.

So when I sit down to write about what I did and where I went and what happened to me in that war, in spite of me it turns out that a good bit of the time I am writing about Sheridan.

I rode at his heels and I carried his flag, and I can see now that you have a strange sort of life when the biggest thing that ever happened to you happens right at the start.

Yet you don't quite know what the really big things are until after they have happened. When you start down the road to war the only thing you can be sure of is that it is going to lead you to a lot of things you didn't expect.

When I went down that road I thought I was running away from something, and it finally turned out that all the time I was going toward something. And what I was going toward was not at all what I had in mind when I set out.

The road led me to Sheridan, and that was important; yet it also led me to a porch in the twilight in a quiet

Virginia town, and on the porch there was a little slip of a girl who laid her hand on my arm and begged me to be careful. In the end, somehow, she meant more than Sheridan did, because if he changed a little of my life, she changed all of it. When I see him I look through that magic glass, and the light on the land has a glow and a color which maybe were not really there. But when I think about her I look ahead instead of back, and I don't need a magic glass because the glow and the color which came with her are real and will never go away.

I know that the road to war, simply because she was on it, finally led me right back to where I started from, only when I got there everything was new and different. Because I had found her, along the road, I also found myself. So perhaps the really important thing about that war was what happened afterward, when people could begin to live again.

. . . Yet it is all mixed up, too, with a little man riding on ahead of me, swinging his hat crunched up in his fist, telling me just by the look and the movement of him that I was a better man than I ever thought I was and that it was going to be a great day in the morning. . . .

Maybe that was part of the truth, too.

2. I HAD TO STAY BEHIND

The town where I lived before the war was built on the east shore of Lake Michigan, right where the river comes down and cuts an opening through the sand bluffs. North and south of the town there are high hills, and the wind off the lake always ruffles through the pines on those hills, so that the place was never really quiet. At night it was almost as if the land was breathing in its sleep, and when the gales blew, the surf beat on the shingle at the foot of the bluffs and made a roar that was like far-off thunder . . . like the crash of guns along a line of battle, I learned later, but in those days I had never heard any guns and I didn't know anything about it.

There was a big sawmill on the flat ground back of the hills and south of the river. Every spring the logs came down, thousands and thousands of them, lumberjacks running along with their cant hooks, big mounds of sawdust growing higher and higher back of the mill. They burned sawdust in the mill's furnaces, but the mill made sawdust faster than it could eat it, so that after a few years the ground around the mill was a queer mixture, half dirt and half sawdust.

All along the river there were big stacks of newly cut lumber, and the clean piny smell of it was always in the air, everywhere in town; you couldn't get away from it, and it smelled so good you wouldn't want to anyway. The schooners kept coming in to take the boards away, but the mill made boards as fast as they could be carried away, and the stacks by the river never seemed to get any smaller.

It was fun, in summer, to climb to the top of one of the bluffs along the lake and pick out a white sail, 'way off on the horizon to the southwest. You could hardly see it, at first. The blue water would be all sparkling with white-caps and glints of sunlight, and for a while you couldn't be dead sure that what you saw was really a sail and not just a wave.

Then it would get bigger, and as the schooner got closer you could see that the sails weren't really as snowy white as they'd looked. They were dirty gray or brown, usually, all patched and stained, and the whole thing looked prettier a long way off than it did close up. That is how it is, I suppose, with a great many things.

It would take hours for the schooner to come in, from the time you first spotted it, and it was pleasant to lie back under the pines on top of the bluff and listen to the wind in the branches, half shut your eyes, and watch the gulls wheeling and dipping out over the shallow water. Every once in a while you'd raise your head and look out to see about your schooner, and there she'd be, spray flying from the bows, sails bellied out smooth and taut.

Then she'd get nearer, and you could see the colored cook walk from the galley to the lee rail to dump a pan of potato peelings, and an officer would be standing by the man at the wheel, hands in his jacket pockets, puffing at a cigar. Finally, when the schooner was right off the harbor entrance, her bows would come around, her sails would shiver and go slack; then they would fill out again as the wind caught her from the other side, and she'd come in past the lighthouse and the breakwater. Then you'd race downhill and run through town to be at the wharf in time to see her tie up.

It was a good place to live, in the summer anyway, although in the winter with the river frozen and big ice floes piled up along the lake shore and no schooners coming or going it was a little dull; and pretty cold, too, with snow three feet deep on level ground and big drifts behind the hills where you could dig great long tunnels and boy-sized rabbit dens.

Altogether I liked our little town of Pine Bay well enough. Yet somehow I always wanted to get away.

Partly, I just wanted to see what lay beyond the lake's horizon, where the white sails vanished, or what was back of us to the east, beyond the deep woods and the lumber camps. But there was more to it than just that. I felt that I could never really begin to be the person I wanted to be until I had got clear out of Pine Bay and gone to some place where nobody knew me.

Pine Bay was a rough, rowdy little town, and although it fascinated me it seemed to have the jump on me, too. I wanted to show that I could stand up to the place; yet as long as I stayed at home I knew I wouldn't get a chance to try.

I lived with my uncle—my folks had died when I was little, and my uncle was a widower, and he took me in. He thought the little town was very wicked, although it didn't bother him very much. He was big and strong and set in his ways, and what went on around him didn't seem to affect him. But he thought it was a bad place for a growing boy, and he tried to hold me out of the life of the town as much as he could.

The mill hands were a tough crowd—and the sailors more so. When the lumberjacks brought the log drives down the river there wasn't a quiet spot within five miles. There were only eight or nine hundred people in all of Pine Bay, but it had half a dozen saloons, all of them handy to the wharves and the mill and all of them doing a land-office business most of the time.

My uncle was the town druggist—"Ebenezer Hayden, Drugs," the sign over his store said. He was also a deacon in the Presbyterian church, and pretty rigid. I wasn't allowed to go downtown after supper, especially not to Front Street, where the wharves and all the saloons and the life and excitement were. I sneaked off, once in a while, but I got tanned when I did, so I was pretty obedient most of the time.

The fact is, I was pretty scared of Uncle Ebenezer. He was solid, with a brick-colored face, clean-shaven except for a fringe of whiskers under the jaw. I thought he was probably the wisest man there was, and very likely the most upright, too. I'd heard different people say how good he was to make a nice home for poor fatherless Bob Hayden—meaning me—and it hardly ever occurred to me to disobey him.

I can see now that he was doing the best he could according to his lights, and he may have been a little extra strict because I wasn't actually his son. Since his own wife had died, he couldn't share the responsibility with anybody. Mrs. Hardy, his housekeeper, was nice. It worried her that I was pale and scrawny and apt to be too sober and she did her best to be good to me, but she didn't really have much to say about my bringing up.

Anyway, the three of us lived in a big frame house on Third Street, halfway up the slope of the hill. From our porch you could look down across the town and see what was going on in the harbor. It was a pretty good home, and I was a lot luckier than a good many people; but I didn't have a strong feeling for the place as home. My daydreams were all about getting away.

It seems now as if time never moved very fast before the Rebs fired on Fort Sumter. Nothing ever seemed to change. The days and the seasons were long, youth itself was long, and it would be forever before I grew up. Besides, folks thought I was kind of frail, and it began to look as if I always would be, which worried me a lot.

Then came the war, and life suddenly moved faster. People kept talking about the changes the war would bring. In my thoughts I got those changes all mixed up with the changes I wanted in my own life, and the first thing I knew I was all impatient—although I didn't know exactly what it was I was impatient about. I just wanted things to happen.

I Had to Stay Behind

When news came in about Fort Sumter they rang the church bells. There was a big war meeting in the town hall, people made speeches, and nobody talked about anything, hardly, but the war.

Our neck of the woods wasn't very thickly settled, and there had never been a militia company around there, but in a few days John Springer came driving over from Lake Ann, which was the county seat, half a dozen miles east of Pine Bay, to look for some recruits.

Mr. Springer, who was a lawyer, was in politics some, and knew everybody in the county. He tied his horse in front of Ole Mason's print shop, got out of his buggy, and went inside to get Mr. Mason to run off a couple of dozen big handbills. He stuck these up on trees and fences and the sides of buildings all over town.

They said: "War! Young Men Wanted!" in type about six inches high, so black it hurt your eyes to look at it. Mr. Springer was enlisting a company he was calling the West Michigan Blue Rifles, to serve for three months. Everybody figured the war would be over in three months, and a lot of young fellows were hot to sign up.

I was, myself, but Uncle Ebenezer put his foot down.

"You're only seventeen, Bob," he said sternly. "You're small for your age. You're frail. Your stomach gets upset easy, and every spring you catch a bad cold. How would you get along sleeping in a tent and living on salt pork and hard bread? Why, you wouldn't last two weeks."

I was afraid he was right, but I mumbled something about how the Rebels had fired on the flag and it was my duty to go. That was a mistake. Duty was something

Uncle Ebenezer knew all about. He was always talking about it as if it was the most sacred word in the language. When I used it, it riled him.

"Duty, sir!" he snapped. "I know what your duty is, and you'll not instruct me in it. Your duty is to stay at home, go on with your studies and apply yourself, and do your best to grow up to be a good, Christian, law-abiding citizen."

We were at the supper table, and he waggled his table knife at me, while Mrs. Hardy looked down at her plate and tried to eat without making any noise, the way she always did when he was reading me a lecture.

"This war——" my uncle began. I felt pretty low, because I knew what was coming. He was a Douglas Democrat, and he hated Mr. Lincoln and the abolitionists. He believed the war was being forced on the South for the benefit of the Republican party. He had said all of that a good many times recently—even the fact that Senator Douglas had come out for the war didn't affect him. Now he said it all over again, and added:

"The Republicans have made this war. Let them fight it."

I thought that was going to be all, but after he ate half a potato cake he was off on a new tack.

"You know who Springer is getting in his company, don't you?" he asked. "He's getting the wild, reckless element from all over the county—the millworkers who get drunk and roister about Front Street on Saturday night, the deck hands who are waiting for the lake to open, the lumberjacks who are tired of the snow out in the woods. That's the sort he's getting, and a fine crew it is."

He was working himself up, and his voice quavered, as it did when he gave testimony in prayer meeting. He went on:

"I'd rather see you in your coffin than see you living with those sinful men, learning their vices and following their godless ways——"

He went on for quite a while, and I could feel myself shrinking.

It didn't seem possible to disobey him. Anyway, I couldn't enlist unless he said I could because anyone under eighteen had to have signed permission from his parents or his guardian. Mr. Springer and everyone else in town knew I wouldn't be eighteen until pretty near Christmas time.

That was that, and I tried to get through the spring as if nothing was happening. The ice went out of the lake, the first schooners came in, the spring log drive came down the river; but somehow things weren't the same any more. Ned Mertz and Tom Benedict, who were my two best friends, signed up in Mr. Springer's company, and all anybody was talking about was the war and how soon the Rebels were going to be licked.

Even the girls didn't seem to be interested in anything except who was enlisting, how soon he would be going, and how fine and brave he was. The town and everything in it began to look very dull. It wasn't fun to go up on the bluffs and watch the sails come in, because you kept thinking about all the things that were going on off beyond the horizon. Instead of seeming grand and romantic, the schooners were just dirty sailboats that never went anywhere except down to Chicago or across to Milwaukee and Sheboygan. It was a pretty bad spring.

After a while Mr. Springer had his whole company enlisted, and along in May they were all assembled at Lake Ann, a full hundred of them. Practically everybody in our town went over to see them off because a lot of the boys had signed up. I hiked over with Ned and Tom, who both tried hard not to show how sorry they were for me. Neither one was more than a year older than I, but they were big and husky, and I felt more like a runt than ever.

When we got to Lake Ann there was a crowd in the public square in front of the courthouse, watching Mr. Springer's company forming near the courthouse door. I shook hands with Ned and Tom and went out in the crowd to watch. I felt mighty blue.

The company had no regular uniforms—they wouldn't get them until they were in camp at Grand Rapids—but they'd managed to dress pretty much alike, with black pants and red lumberjack shirts and black slouch hats, and they looked pretty good.

Mr. Springer did have a uniform, a fancy one, gray with black facings, that made him look big and important. Some committee of ladies presented him with a flag and he made a speech, saying how his boys would protect that flag with their lives and bring it back unstained by dishonor. There were more speeches, and the Reverend Brinkerhoff gave a prayer—a long prayer. Everybody stood there with bared heads in the wind, which was kind of cool, while he talked about these young heroes and asked God to bless them. You could hear women crying, trying not to make too much noise about it. I stood there hating Reverend Brinkerhoff and Mr. Springer and everybody in his company, including Ned and Tom.

Then the prayer was over. The Silver Cornet Band began to play a quickstep, Mr. Springer was barking commands, and the company marched over to the vacant lot by Mullins's Livery Stable, where there were a dozen or more wagons to take them to Grand Rapids. It was a good fifty miles, and they'd have to camp out along the way.

It seemed as if half the people in the county were jammed around the wagons as the boys piled in. People were calling out goodbye, laughing and crying together, handing up baskets of fried chicken and cakes and things for the boys to eat along the way. The band kept on playing although there was so much of a hubbub you could hardly hear it.

At last the drivers cracked their whips. You could hear townsmen calling out, important-like: "Stand back! Let 'em turn——" Then the wagons went creaking off, lumbering down the hill and rumbling over the Cold Creek bridge, and we couldn't see them any more.

I had a pretty gone feeling when they disappeared, and the walk back home seemed long. That night at supper my uncle asked me where I'd been. I told him, and he looked thoughtful.

"Well, they're gone," he said at last. "I hope they'll be all that's needed. Anyway, they'll be back before the summer ends."

As it turned out, they weren't. When their three-month term was up the regiment was off in Virginia somewhere. Most of the men re-enlisted for the full three years, and things were a lot different before what was left of that regiment ever saw Michigan again.

But even if they had returned in three months I wouldn't have been there to see them. For by that time I was in the army myself.

3. THE ROAD TO WAR

In a way it was mostly Otis Cleverdun's fault.

Otis was a sandy-haired, skinny fellow my age, who lived on a farm a couple of miles out of town. I didn't know him very well, but in a town that small everybody knew everybody at least a little. I used to see Otis once in a while and we got along all right the little we did see each other.

It was around the end of July, a hot afternoon with no wind. I had gone down to the steamboat dock to pick up a package of stuff that had come up on the side-wheeler from Chicago. While I was there I saw Otis, sitting on a piling, looking down at the water.

"What're you doing here?" I asked him.

"Just loafin'," he said. He kept on looking at the water, and then he said: "Mr. Springer's company was in that fight at Bull Run."

"How'd you know?"

"A fellow here got a Detroit paper. He was reading it out loud, a few minutes ago."

We'd had the news about Bull Run several days ago,

but we hadn't had any details yet. I hated it when Otis told me that, and it wasn't because I was thinking about any of the men in the company getting killed or worrying whether Tom and Ned were all right. I was just jealous. I kept thinking: They've been in a battle. They're heroes. They know what it's like. They did something I wasn't allowed to do. I missed it all. I stood there feeling sorry for myself.

"Some of the boys was wounded," said Otis. That woke me up a little, and I asked him who. He named three or four names but none of them were people I knew very well. Ned and Tom were all right.

Then Otis said:

"They say it's going to be a long war now. The state's enlisting new regiments for three years."

A seagull went paddling by on the surface of the water, looking up at us sort of mean-like, and Otis watched it for a while. Then he said:

"I'm going to enlist."

I stared at him. Old man Cleverdun was hard-shell, just as tough a nut to crack as Uncle Ebenezer. Otis was no older than I was, and he wasn't a bit bigger or stronger.

"You can't," I said. "Your pa won't let you."

"My pa isn't going to know anything about it until it's too late," said Otis.

"But you're under eighteen, and they won't take you unless you got his consent."

Otis gave me a funny, wise look from under the brim of his straw hat.

"I know a way around that," he said.

"You can't tell 'em you're eighteen when you aren't," I

insisted. "That's government. You could get in bad trouble."

He just wagged his head and repeated: "I know a way."

Maybe he did—Otis was kind of a schemer. But I didn't see how he was going to manage it. All of a sudden I realized that I was scared to find out.

"You just going to run away?" I asked him.

"Yep."

"You got to go to Grand Rapids to enlist, don't you?"

"Yep."

"How you going to get there?"

"Walk. You can do it in three or four days or a little over. Most likely you can hook a ride part of the way. Once you get down past Bear River, there's always lumber camp wagons going after supplies. They'll usually let you ride."

I wanted to prove he was wrong. 'Way down inside, something seemed to be telling me: If Otis could do it, so could you—and you just don't dare to try!

"What's to keep your pa from getting in his buckboard and going after you and bringing you back?" I asked. (Old Man Cleverdun would try it—and so would Uncle Ebenezer. And do it, too.)

"I got that all figured," said Otis. "I'm going to leave a note for him. I'm going to say I've gone off to join the army. Only what I'm going to say is that I'm shipping across the lake to Milwaukee on a lumber hooker. Everybody knows it's easy to do that if you get on the good side of the mate. So if Pa tries to catch me he'll go looking in the wrong direction, and by the time he's found out it'll be too late. Once you've enlisted they can't get you out. I looked it up."

He was triumphant about it, and I thought: I believe Otis knows what he's talking about. It could be done, if you dared to try.

"When you going?" I asked.

"Tomorrow night, after Pa's gone to bed. I'll go out my window onto the shed roof and, off that, it's an easy jump to the ground. Shucks, I'll be fifteen miles on my way before he knows I'm gone."

"What you going to do nights?"

"Hike—anyhow, until I get past Bear River. I don't want anyone to see me until it's too late for Pa to catch up with me."

"I mean, how you going to sleep?"

"Oh, sleep in the daytime. In woods and so on."

He was pretty lofty, with his "and so on." I said:

"Out in the open?"

"Of course."

I was doubtful.

"I catch cold awful easy," I said. "I don't see how I could sleep out. I'd catch my death of cold."

"What you going to do in the army, if you can't sleep outdoors?" Otis asked scornfully. I said: "Well, that's so."

"Besides," said Otis, "it's summer. It isn't *cold*."

Once more I said: "Well, that's so."

Otis gave me a sidelong look from under his hat. Little specks of sunlight came down through the loose weave of the straw brim and mixed with the freckles on his cheeks.

"You coming?" he asked.

I knew what was the matter with me; I was just plain

afraid. Afraid to disobey Uncle Ebenezer, afraid to get out of the quiet little groove I was in, afraid of the war and the army and of everything that lay ahead of me. It didn't seem as if I was going to get over being afraid right away, either, but I thought: Maybe if I act as if I'm not afraid, if I just pretend that everything's all right, things will be different. I've got to pretend I'm man enough to face things, even if I'm not. And I heard myself saying:

"Yes."

Otis didn't seem surprised. He asked:

"What time do folks at your house go to bed?"

"Oh, I don't know. Pretty early."

That was safe enough. Everybody in town, except for a few along Front Street, was in bed long before ten.

Otis wagged his head. He was full of business.

"Look," he said, "you know where that clump of maples is, down by the road, just after you pass our house? I'll wait for you down there about half past nine tomorrow night. Don't say anything out loud when you come up because our house isn't far from the road and sound carries awful far at night." (As if I didn't know that!) "And be sure to bring something to eat, because we're going to be four or five days on the road, and we don't want to have to ask at farmhouses."

I said I would. Neither one of us had a watch and how we were going to tell when it was nine-thirty I didn't quite know, but that was all right. Otis jumped down off the piling and said: "Tomorrow night, now—you be there!" And away he went.

It seemed as if there was a lot of planning to do. At first I was going to wait until everybody was in bed and just slip out, leaving the same kind of note Otis was leaving, but I could see that wouldn't do. Uncle Ebenezer lived right in town and knew how those schooners operated. They'd load up in the daytime, and either put out before sunset or wait until next day. Sometimes they came in at night, but they hardly ever left at night; if I went away after dark leaving a note saying I'd gone off on a schooner, my uncle would know right away it wasn't so.

I couldn't just say I was going to enlist and leave it at that because unless I laid some sort of false trail anybody would know I was going to go to Grand Rapids. If I knew my uncle, he'd hire a rig and go after me. Even if he didn't find me on the way, it'd be simple for him just to go to the recruiting office and wait for me, and if he did that I was licked because, after all, I was still under eighteen.

Then at last I had an idea.

I got the package of stuff from the steamboat, took it back to the store, and told Uncle Ebenezer that I wanted to go down to Mr. Naylor's place next day and pick blackberries on shares. The berries grew wild on the cutover land in Mr. Naylor's back pasture, which was off south of town a ways, and people often arranged with Mr. Naylor to pick on shares—that is, you'd pick the berries on his land, and at the end of the day you'd stop at his back door and give him half of what you'd picked. That way he got his berries picked free and you got a nice bucketful for yourself, free except for the day's work, which wasn't hard work especially. Every summer Mrs. Hardy put up jam and preserves, so Uncle Ebenezer thought it was a fine idea and told me to go ahead.

There was a big three-master tied up down by the mill,

the *Betsy Johnston,* getting the last of her load that afternoon. She figured to sail sometime next morning, so I could pretend she was the vessel I was taking. (If tomorrow turned out to be so windless she couldn't put out, that would spoil my story, but that was a chance I had to take.) That night, after supper, I went up to my room, got my pencil and tablet, and wrote a note to my uncle. I said:

Dear Uncle Ebenezer: I did not go berrying down to Mr. Naylor's today. Instead I am shipping out on the Betsy Johnston. *She is going to Milwaukee, and one of the men on the* Betsy Johnston *says the 5th Wisconsin Infantry is enlisting there and when I get to Milwaukee I am going to join that regiment. If they will take me. I am doing this because I think it is my duty to my country and my flag, and I know you think otherwise but I still feel it is my duty. I am sorry to be disobedient and hurt your feelings but it is my duty.*

Goodbye, from Bob

Some of the note was actually true. That is, I had heard men say that that particular regiment was taking on men in Milwaukee, and I thought it would make it sound more real to put in the name of the regiment.

At first I didn't know where to leave this note, because of course I didn't want Uncle Ebenezer to read it until the next evening. Then I remembered that every night after supper my uncle would get down a big book called somebody's *Exposition of the Scriptures* and read it for a while. I decided I would hide the note in that book.

Since I was supposed to be going berrying, I would have my rough clothes and boots on, fit for a long hike and sleeping out of doors, so that part would be all right. I stuffed an extra pair of socks in one pocket, and I made up my mind I would take my money.

One thing I will say for Uncle Ebenezer, he was not a skinflint. I had been working in the store regularly that spring, and he paid me a dollar and a half every week, which a lot of men would not have done, seeing I was practically his son and had lived all my life in his house. I had a little stock of half dollars in my dresser drawer, which I tied up in a clean bandanna handkerchief and put in my pocket along with the extra socks.

It was easy. The next morning after breakfast I slipped into the parlor, put my goodbye note into the *Exposition of the Scriptures*, and, when Uncle Ebenezer left for the store, I went into the kitchen for the two big tin buckets for the blackberries. Mrs. Hardy made me a couple of sandwiches, and pretty soon I got out of the house and started off.

The way I was going I walked right past the drugstore. I didn't see my uncle and I don't know if he saw me or not. A little farther on I came to Snell's market, where I bought a couple of pounds of cheese and a lot of crackers. I didn't know what else to take, but he had a box of salt herrings on the counter so I bought some of those. I put all of my stuff in one of the buckets, nested it inside the other bucket, hooked my arm through the bail, and off I went.

But instead of going on south toward Naylor's farm, I made a circle as soon as I got out of town, went 'way up on top of the hill to the north, and came out along the highest part of the bluff overlooking the lake. There was a place in a pine thicket there where I had played a lot in years past. It was out of the way and nobody ever came there. I figured I would simply hide out there until night.

It was nice up there. The bluff was at least three hundred feet high, and very steep. You could see for miles up and down the big blue lake, with the yellow sand running along the shore as far as you could see. I put my buckets under a tree, lay down, and looked out, and felt pretty good. I told myself I felt good because I was doing my duty and serving my country—that is, I was if the army would take me: I still wasn't quite sure about Otis's plan for beating the rule on the eighteen years business—but down inside I knew that what I really was happy about was just getting away and going off on my own. It seemed as if from now on everything was going to be exciting.

The day was warm, with a pleasant wind, steady and not very strong, and I dozed a little. Once, somewhere around noon, I looked out and saw the *Betsy Johnston* standing out into the lake, so the note I had left for Uncle Ebenezer would hold up. The schooner went off toward the west, looking clumsy with her deckload of lumber, while I watched her go and wondered if I shouldn't really have done what I was pretending to have done—crossed the lake to try to join that Wisconsin regiment. But it was too late now. I leaned back, ate my sandwiches, and waited for the long day to end.

It seemed as if the sun would never go down but at last it did. The western sky over the lake was all warm and soft and peaceful, faint red and gold turning into pale blue, with a greenish tint getting mixed up in it somehow. I knew there'd be fair weather for a day or so. That was good, because if it rained I would probably get sick and that might keep me from enlisting. Then I wondered how anybody who got sick as easy as I did would get along in the army. It looked like a bad sort of gamble and I wondered how far you could carry this business of pretending to be braver and stronger than you really were.

The last color left the sky, finally, and in the pine thicket it was dark as the inside of your pocket, so I picked up my buckets and started.

It was no trouble circling around the edge of town until I hit the main road and tramped east, stopping now and then to listen and make sure nobody was coming. Uncle Ebenezer would have read my note by this time, and I could imagine him—big, strong, and angry, stamping about the house, berating me. It just didn't seem possible that he wouldn't catch on to my trick and come along the road any minute, one hand reaching out for my coat collar. If I didn't keep looking back, I could almost feel his hand clutching me.

So I jumped about five feet when a voice at the side of the road said "Hi!" I turned, and there was a shadowy form coming out of a clump of trees—Otis. I said "Oh!" and told him he had scared me, and he told me not to make so much noise. We didn't say much until we had walked about a mile. After a while Otis asked what I thought I I was going to do with those big buckets in the army. I realized there was no need to lug them any farther, so we made a little bundle out of the cheese and crackers and salt fish and hid the buckets under a tree.

We kept walking. By-and-by we had to stop talking so as to save our wind, but we kept plodding along for hours.

The Road to War

It was dark and we never met a soul. I kept stopping to listen, but I never did hear anything. At last we got to Lake Ann. We walked right on through the town. It was sort of spooky, with everything dark and not a sound anywhere; somehow it didn't look like any place I'd ever been in before, or like a place where anybody really lived.

Nobody saw us or heard us. Even the dogs didn't wake up and bark at us. We kept on and on until my feet began to feel heavy, and then I realized that I could see the outlines of trees and hills a little. There was a faint haze or mist in the fields, and as the sky grew lighter everything looked mysterious. It seemed even quieter than it had in the middle of the night.

Otis said we'd gone fifteen miles and it was time to stop, so we turned off the road at a place where there was a little brook, sat down, and cooled our feet in the water. Then we ate some crackers and fish, and the half of a mince pie Otis had brought along, and leaned back against a big beech tree to talk things over. We were going to go on for another hour or so, but we were pretty tired. We were out of sight of the road where we were, so at last we slid down a little and stretched out. I was still worrying about Uncle Ebenezer overtaking us, and about catching cold from lying on the bare ground, but while I worried we went off to sleep.

★

4.   NEW STORE CLOTHES

It was a long hike, but somehow it went a lot easier than I thought it would. We took four days for it, hiking all night and sleeping all day. We slept anywhere we could find. Once we burrowed into an old haystack behind a barn and were snug as could be, but the other times we just flopped under the trees. The weather was good, and although I was stiff and sore every time we woke up I didn't catch a cold. I couldn't understand why not.

There was just one thing that really bothered us. Our feet got awfully sore. We'd soak them every time we came to a stream, but we finally found out that that isn't a good thing to do except when you're all through walking and can sleep afterward. If you put your socks and shoes back on and start off again, pretty soon your feet hurt worse than ever. We both got blisters, and toward the last I was limping a good deal. Otis took his shoes and stockings off and carried them, stumping along barefooted.

We were dirty and lame when we finally got to Grand Rapids. We had eaten the last of our food, and down inside I was beginning to wonder if I had been so smart after all.

"In the army you have to walk an awful lot," I said.

"Maybe you get used to it," said Otis.

"I hope I get used to it soon, then. This is pretty bad."

We sat down on a little bank by the road, while Otis put his shoes on. It was morning, and we were just coming in through the edge of town. I wiggled my toes inside my shoes, and Otis said: "Well, we might as well keep going." So we started off again. I began to wonder where we would find the place to join the army.

Then we heard something, not far off. A bugle was blatting away, sounding thin and tinny in the morning air. We listened and looked around, trying to judge where the noise was coming from. We kept on walking, until we came over a little rise in the ground where we could see an open field off to the right, with long rows of one-story buildings at one side and a lot of sheds and racks full of hay running along behind them. Men in blue uniforms were moving in and out of the sheds. In the field beyond we could see a troop of cavalry trotting along on the open ground.

There was an officer riding out in front, with a bugler riding beside him. As we watched, the bugler sounded a few notes and the whole line of mounted men swung around, trotting along in a solid column, four men abreast. I thought I had never seen anything so grand.

"You know," said Otis, "those fellows there. They're soldiers, all right. But when they go someplace, they *ride*. They don't have to do it all on foot."

The way my feet felt, that sounded wonderful.

"The only trouble," Otis went on, "is that a horse is an awful lot of trouble to take care of. But maybe they have stable hands or somebody to do all of that."

I didn't care how much trouble it would be. I only knew that moving column of men on horses looked grander than anything I had ever seen. I wanted to belong to something like that.

"Did you ever ride a horse?" Otis was asking me. I shook my head. I'd never been on a horse in my life.

"Well," he said, "maybe they teach you."

Pretty soon we came to a gate in the whitewashed fence that set the camp off from the road. There was a cabin near it, and a soldier stood in the gate with a little short gun in his hands. We walked up and Otis asked: "Who's the man in charge here?"

The soldier looked us over, very superior. I must admit we weren't very impressive—neither of us over five feet five, nor weighing more than one hundred and thirty pounds, both of us dusty and footsore, me with my dark hair leaking every which way out from under my hat, Otis with a great tear in one sleeve. The soldier was big and I thought he looked magnificent. I know now that he was a very green recruit, but I didn't know it then and I felt very insignificant, which was exactly what he wanted.

"Right here at this gate, I'm the man in charge," he said. He spat tobacco juice in the ditch, and then said: "What do you want?"

I said: "We want to enlist."

He looked us over, very carefully, as if he didn't exactly believe what he saw. He shook his head.

"They'd never take you," he said.

"Why not?" Otis demanded.

The soldier spat again.

"You're too puny," he said. "You couldn't stand the gaff.

The cavalry wants *men*. Especially this regiment. This is a
crack regiment. We got two whole companies of lumberjacks. We got a lieutenant colonel who's high up in the
Great Western Railway. We got——"

Inside the cabin someone yelled "Sentry!" real sharp.
The soldier had been sort of lounging while he talked to us,
but now he stiffened up in a hurry, bumping the butt of his
piece against one anklebone as he did so. He called out
"Yessir!" real meek.

Out of the hut came a slim little man with a trim black
beard. He wore skin-tight pants of light blue with a yellow stripe down the side, tucked into big boots like a
pirate's. His jacket was short, hardly coming down below
his waist, and dark blue, almost as tight as the pants, with
a row of brass buttons in front. He had a neat little forage
cap pulled down over his eyes, and shoulder straps
stitched with heavy gold thread. (He was a first lieutenant,
although for all I knew just then he might have been a
major general.) Around his waist he wore a heavy belt,
with a saber in its scabbard hanging from it, on the left
side, by two straps. He didn't have it hooked up, and when
he walked, the lower end of the scabbard trailed along
the ground; it looked sort of negligent and easy, and for
some reason that one little careless touch made him seem
even more trim and dapper.

"You're not supposed to carry on a conversation with
visitors at the gate," said the officer sharply to the sentry.
"Stand at port arms when they come up to you. Stand at
attention when *I* come up."

"Yessir," said the sentry. He hurriedly swung his carbine
up diagonally across his chest, holding it with both hands.

41

Before he had that move finished he swung around and tried to stand at attention facing the officer, with the gun butt grounded beside his right heel. He sort of went into a flurry and almost knocked himself over doing it. He got red and looked flustered and unhappy. Otis and I enjoyed it very much.

The officer looked at the sentry for a minute without saying anything, and the sentry seemed to shrink considerably. Then the officer turned to us.

"What do you want, boys?" he asked. His voice was pleasant.

Otis couldn't seem to find his tongue, so I spoke up: "Well, sir, we want to join the army."

The officer nodded.

"This is the 2d Michigan Cavalry," he said. "Go on up to that building there, go in the first door, and they'll take care of you." He pointed to a long, low building built of raw pine boards, standing about a hundred feet away. He looked us over briefly.

"Got your parents' consent?" he asked.

Otis spoke up. "We don't need it," he said stoutly.

"Oh?" A faint smile touched the corners of the lieutenant's mouth. "All right. Did you ever ride a horse?"

I shook my head, and the officer shrugged.

"Neither has anybody else," he said. "Well, we can take care of that. Go on up there and they'll fix you up."

He went back into the little hut. Otis and I looked scornfully at the sentry and walked up the path to the door the officer had pointed out. There was a short flight of steps, and when we got to them Otis stopped me.

"Now," he said, "we'll fix it about that age business."

He pulled a stub pencil and a sheet of paper out of one pocket, tore the paper in half, wrote the figure "18" on each piece, and gave one to me.

"Take off one shoe and put this in the bottom of it," he directed. He sat down on the steps and began to unlace one of his own shoes. I was puzzled, but I did what he told me to do. When I had laid the paper on the sole of my shoe, Otis had me put the shoe on and lace it up, while he did the same. When we stood up, he asked me:

"Now, what're you standing on?"

I didn't know what he was getting at. "On my feet, of course."

Otis shook his head. "Gosh, but you're stupid. I mean, what've you got in that shoe? What did you just put in it?"

I felt like telling him I had just put my foot in it, but I could see that wouldn't do. "A piece of paper," I said.

I thought Otis was going to blow up. He got hold of himself, and asked:

"What did I write on that piece of paper?"

I said: "Eighteen."

"Yeah. Eighteen. And when you're standing on it, you're *over* it, aren't you?"

I nodded. Otis looked triumphant.

"So," he said. "When the man asks you how old you are, what do you tell him?"

A great light dawned.

"I'm over eighteen!"

"Sure you are! That way, you're not lying to the government. You *are* over eighteen, and you can say so. Now let's go inside."

43

It was a lot easier than I had thought it would be, although nothing seemed to happen very fast. There were a dozen or more fellows in civilian clothes, sitting around in a big room. At one end a sergeant sat behind a table with pen and ink and a set of printed forms. After a while it was our turn to answer his questions—what were our names, where did we live, who were our nearest relatives, and so on. When he asked our ages, we both said we were over eighteen. He stared at us for a moment, then nodded slowly, as much as to say that he had heard that before and knew all about it.

"Eighteen it is," he said, writing it down.

We waited for a long time, while more young fellows came in. Somewhere along toward noon we all were shooed out into an open yard and lined up in a long row. After a while a couple of officers came up and walked along the line, looking us over pretty carefully. One of them kept addressing the other as "Surgeon," although if he was a doctor—and I found out later he really was—he certainly didn't give us much of an examination. He just looked us over as he walked along.

He spotted one fellow with a withered arm and pulled him out of line, feeling of his arm carefully. Then he told him he would have to go home. The fellow went away looking unhappy. The doctor pulled out a skinny, hollow-chested man, thumped him a few times, put his ear to the man's chest, frowned, and shook his head, and that man also had to go away. All the rest of us were passed.

The officer was a burly, thickset man with a bristly black mustache and a proud, pouter pigeon sort of look to him. He had quite a few medals on his chest and he moved as if he was pretty important. After he and the doctor had looked us all over, he stood out in front, facing us.

"I'm Lieutenant Colonel Davies," he said. He had a red nose and seamy red cheeks that made him look like some of the hard-drinking lakers you'd see hanging around the saloons on Front Street, back home.

"Hold up your right hands," he ordered. A sergeant who had been standing behind the officer stepped forward and read off an oath, a few words at a time, which we had to repeat every time he paused. When that was over, Colonel Davies looked at us.

"You're in the army now, men," he said. It was the first time anybody ever called me "men," and I was quite impressed. "Obey your officers, do your duty, keep out of trouble, and you'll get along fine. Sergeant, take 'em away."

The colonel and the surgeon disappeared, and the sergeant herded us over toward another building. As we went, one of the men asked: "Who is that old coot, anyhow?"

"You heard him say," said the sergeant. "He's boss of the regiment, that's who he is. When he tells you to do something, you better jump." He paused a minute and then added: "When anybody tells you to do something, you better jump. Most of all, you better jump when *I* tell you to do something."

"Who says we got to jump for you?" someone asked.

So far I hadn't paid much attention to the sergeant, but all at once he seemed to be somebody to look at. He was short and wiry, with dark leathery skin. He had fine wrinkles at the outer corners of his eyes, as if he had

45

peered into hot sunlight a good deal, and there were sharp lines from his nostrils to the ends of his mouth. He might have been a mate on a lumber hooker, or a camp boss running a log drive in the spring; whatever and wherever he was, I began to realize, he would be apt to be in charge of things.

He walked over to the fellow who had spoken and he said, real gentle-like:

"Partner, you just try *not* jumping some time when I tell you to do something and you'll find out who says."

The fellow was a big lout, a head taller than the sergeant, and he was not impressed. He said:

"You don't look to me like anybody I got to jump for."

The sergeant said "No?" sort of wistfully, and then he hit the big man in the stomach, very hard. The big man bent over and the sergeant hit him on the mouth. There was a sort of windmill of flying arms and fists, then the big fellow was staggering backward, off balance. The sergeant moved in, hit him once more, and the big fellow fell down, whacking his head against the steps of the barracks. He was out cold.

The sergeant looked at us and tugged at the visor of his cap. He asked: "Anybody else want to know who says you got to jump?" Nobody said anything. Two soldiers carrying buckets of water for some cleaning detail came around the corner just then, and the sergeant took one of the buckets. He sloshed the water over the unconscious man, who gasped and sputtered and more or less came to, and then gave the empty bucket back to the soldier and told him: "When he sits up, tell him to come on over to the QM shed. We're going to draw uniforms."

New Store Clothes

We drew uniforms, and I was one of the few who made out all right. The army made its uniforms in just three sizes—small, medium, and large—and the man behind the counter just flung them out without looking at the man who was drawing, so most of the boys had to do a lot of swapping around afterward. I was lucky. I was small, and I drew a small-size uniform that fitted me pretty well. After a while we were taken over to one of the barracks, a long, low building with little windows on one side and two tiers of wide shelves on the other. The shelves were bunks, wide enough for two men at a time, so everybody was picking bunk mates. Otis and I were bunkies, of course. We all got straw from a pile outside, filled the bunks, and spread blankets over them. It looked as if they might be all right for sleeping.

Then we went around to the cook shack, where each of us got a tin plate with boiled potatoes, a slice of boiled beef, a thick slice of bread, and a cup of black coffee. I was going to ask if we didn't get any milk to put in our coffee, but I didn't like the look in the sergeant's eye so I didn't ask, which was probably just as well. We ate standing up, resting our plates and cups on a narrow ledge that had been built along one wall of our barracks. I didn't think the food was especially good but I was awfully hungry and ate it all.

Then the sergeant took us outside in a big yard, where the dirt was packed down hard. He lined us all up in a row, and I took a look down the line. We were all in uniform now, with the light pants and the short blue jackets and the trim little forage caps, yet somehow we didn't quite look like soldiers. We just looked like a lot of boys

47

who had put new store clothes on, and it was easy to see that we had never been in uniform before.

I didn't like that. I wanted to look like the sergeant, or the little officer we'd seen down by the gate, or even like big husky Colonel Davies. They moved around as if they'd never worn anything but those uniforms. They looked trim and neat and kind of careless at the same time, and I wondered how long it would take before we'd look like that, too.

It turned out that it was going to take quite a while. We spent most of the rest of that day just learning how to stand up straight.

5. THE MAKING OF A TROOPER

Like a green country bumpkin I had supposed we would start right out that first afternoon riding around on horses and brandishing our sabers. I was wrong. Cavalrymen had to do a lot of walking, it seemed, and when they walked the army wanted them to do it just so.

The army was mostly the little sergeant, those days. Joss Pettit, his name was, and when he told us to, we jumped, with no more back talk. He said we weren't fit to get on real, self-respecting cavalry horses yet, because first we had to learn a little about soldiering, which he was going to teach us.

He'd begin by barking: "Take the position of a soldier!"

We found out that meant to stand stiff, heels together, head up, chest out, thumbs touching the seams of our pants. I'd never heard of anybody standing that way before, but that was the way the army liked it. When the sergeant had us all standing that way he taught us how to walk.

It seemed that when a soldier wanted to get from one place to another he couldn't just mosey over there. No indeed. He had to do it very precise and regular, turning square corners, picking up his feet just so, and always starting out by moving his left foot first. It was pretty ridiculous, I thought, but it was simple enough, and anyhow Joss Pettit set a lot of store by it.

Simple as it was, some of the boys had a hard time catching on. There was one fellow named Peterson, or Peterkin, or something—we all called him Pete—who never could manage to step off with his left foot first, or to keep time when Sergeant Pettit would trot along saying "Hup! Hup! Hup!" Finally the sergeant took him in hand.

"You know the difference between hay and straw, do you?" the sergeant asked him. Pete blinked at him. He'd lived on a farm all of his nineteen or twenty years, so of course he could tell hay from straw. He nodded.

"Go down to the stables," said the sergeant, "and fetch me a handful of hay and a handful of straw. On the double!"

We had already learned that "on the double" meant to run, and Pete set off. When he came back Sergeant Pettit was waiting with a couple of pieces of twine. He tied the bunch of hay to Pete's left foot and the straw to his right foot. Then he stood back and looked him over.

"The rest of you watch this," the sergeant called out. "Maybe some of you need the same lesson, and if you do we'll easy get some more hay and straw."

Then he waggled his finger under Pete's nose.

"Now," he said, "when I say 'hay!' you move the foot that's got the hay tied to it, and when I say 'straw!' you move the straw-foot, and keep on doing it. Got it?"

Pete was sort of red and embarrassed, but he nodded.

"Remember," said the sergeant, "when I holler 'march!' you start off with the hay-foot. Now——"

He gave the command, and as Pete began to march the sergeant trotted along beside him, yelling: "Hay-foot! Straw-foot! Hay-foot! Straw-foot! Hup! Hup! Hup!"

He marched Pete around in a little square, while the rest of us watched. Once somebody guffawed, but Pettit growled:

"Anybody thinks it's so funny can come out here and wear some of these barnyard decorations himself."

After that nobody had anything to say. But for days afterward, when we were getting drilled, the sergeant would chant the hay-foot-straw-foot thing, and he would make the rest of us say it with him. After a while, everybody knew which foot was which.

One day, while we were taking a breather between exercises, somebody mumbled that he couldn't see why we had to do all of this foot drill when we had signed up to ride horses. Pettit's eyes got narrow, as if he were out in the Indian country peering across a glaring sunlit plain at something repulsive. We were such revolting straw-feet, he told us, that no decent war horse would let us get within a rod of him. Besides, even when we were fit to learn cavalry business, what we'd get would be mostly dragoon drill.

Dragoon drill? We had just sense enough not to say "What is that?" He saw we were puzzled, and unbent enough to explain.

"Dragoons," said the sergeant, "are cavalrymen, only they do most of their fighting on foot. They ride horses so they can get where they want to go and get there fast, but generally they don't stay on 'em to fight. It'd take a forty-acre lot for two cavalry regiments to fight if everybody stayed mounted, and where we're going there aren't very many forty-acre lots. There are——"

In the army there is always some squarehead with a question, and one of these asked: "Where *are* we going?" Pettit gave him a dirty look, and went on:

"Pretty soon you'll be drawing carbines, and the government don't buy them just so's you'll look pretty carrying 'em. You're expected to shoot with 'em, and you stand a lot better chance of hitting what you're shooting at if you're on the ground instead of in the saddle when you shoot."

Somebody asked: "How about swords? Aren't they going to give us swords? What do we do with them?"

Sergeant Pettit swore.

"*Sabers!* Not swords. Sabers. Mostly, you trip over 'em. Or, when you're riding, they bang against your horse's side and scare him so he goes off into a gallop when you don't want him to. Sometimes, when you swing 'em, you cut your horse's ears off. Or hit your partner in the head."

This was disillusioning, because my mind was full of pictures of brilliant cavalry charges with everybody waving long swords, which I thought would be very exciting. Apparently everybody else felt the same way, and the sergeant seemed to know it because all at once he grinned.

"Oh, sometimes you'll use your sabers," he said. "There'll be mounted actions once in a while, when you're on patrol and such. But in a fight like that a revolver is a lot more use than a saber. I don't know if this regiment is going to draw revolvers, but if you ever get one hang onto it."

None of this was quite what I'd been expecting, somehow. I'd been in the cavalry two weeks now, and I hadn't even seen any horses—except a few at a distance. Now this tough little sergeant was saying we'd fight on foot, and was implying that our sabers (when we finally got them) would just be a nuisance.

When we got our horses, at last, I had another surprise coming to me.

A big drove of horses was brought in, one morning after breakfast, and we went down to the picket ropes right away. There were officers and civilians all around, but as usual it seemed to be Sergeant Pettit who was in charge of things.

The horses looked small and a little ragged.

"They're Canucks," one man was saying. "Government brings 'em over from Canada. They say they're a French breed. Don't look like much, but they got a lot of endurance. And they'll eat almost anything."

However all of that might be, each of us drew a horse. Right then and there I learned that Otis was all wrong when he supposed that the army had stable boys to do the dirty work. That work was all done by the troopers— meaning us—and we were not long in finding out that it was the most important single thing on the program, day in and day out.

Sergeant Pettit explained. That little man did enjoy laying down the law.

"A good trooper," said the sergeant, "looks after his horse before he looks after himself. If he's in *my* company, he does whether he's a good trooper or a bad one, or he gets chewed out something awful. . . .

"You got to see to it that your horse gets something to eat before you fix something for yourself. You got to get your horse bedded down for the night before you fix your own place to sleep. That means get the saddle off of him, clean him, bring some forage for him, and give him his water. You got to do all that before you make your own bivouac. If the supply wagon don't come up and the forage rack is empty, a good trooper will find something for his horse regardless, even if he has to steal it from somebody."

He fixed us with a sharp eye, which was something he enjoyed doing.

"You're no better than your horse. If he gets worn out and can't carry you, you're no good at all. You go into Company Q then, and you get all the camp police to do, and you're no use to anybody. You take care of your horse and he'll take care of you."

It turned out that the sergeant was very particular about the way we saddled our horses. If he had taken pains with our foot drill, he took five times as many pains with anything that affected our horses.

"Don't just throw that saddle blanket on!" he would storm. "See that wrinkle there? Inside of ten miles your horse'd have a saddle sore, and then, my friend, you'd have to get off and walk. Also"—he glared at all of us—"also, you'd take the saddle off and carry it all the rest of the way, and you'd lead your horse while you're doing it. And that night you'd explain to *me* why your horse got a saddle sore."

The Making of a Trooper

For a while I thought we were going to spend all the rest of our lives just taking care of horses. I learned how to use a brush and comb, and I learned how to put grain in a nose bag and put the nose bag on the horse so that he could eat out of it. Also, I learned how to use a pitchfork. But while all of this was happening, what was most important of all was that I began to learn something about horses—in particular, about the little chestnut named Red that had been assigned to me, to be "my horse" from now on. He was undersized, same as I was, so I called him *Big* Red to make up for it.

It had never occurred to me that you could get acquainted with a horse. I had never had a thing to do with horses before. At first I was pretty uncertain about it, and I guess Big Red felt the same way about me. But as I got used to him he got used to me, and the first thing I knew we were actually friends.

Red caught on quick that I was the soldier who took care of him, and when the squad went out to the picket ropes he would look for me, almost as if he was saying hello to me. He reminded me some of Uncle Ebenezer's big cat, Ricky, who never had much to say to you but would sidle up against you once in a while just by way of saying that he knew you were his friend. Red was that way. After the first few days, he'd give a little nicker when he saw me coming down the stable line. A few times, I put a little sugar on a piece of hardtack and gave it to him, so he would nuzzle me every time I came up, after that, to see if I had anything for him.

I got so I'd talk to him while I was grooming him. At first I was just trying to soothe him so he'd stand still and let me work, but before long I was really talking to him, telling him stuff just as if he was somebody I'd known a long time. It probably would have sounded kind of silly if anybody had listened, but along the picket ropes nobody paid any attention. I wouldn't have cared much, anyhow. I'd never really felt as if I could talk to anybody much—I mean, to talk the way you want to talk when you're trying to get things off your chest. Having Red around was almost as good as having a real friend. Better, in lots of ways; I thought more of Red than I did of most people I'd known.

Otis was right, of course, when he said that taking care of a horse was a lot of work, but I didn't mind it. Taking care of Red was fun, not work. The army can be an awfully lonely place—extra lonely, I suppose, just because there are always hundreds of people around you but no one you really know—but as long as I had Red I didn't seem to mind it. I began to see why Joss Pettit insisted that a cavalryman didn't amount to much without his horse.

Our 2d Michigan regiment had been about three-quarters full when Otis and I joined up, and some of the companies had been doing mounted drill for several weeks. From the new recruits that came in when we did, they sifted out about twenty who had never ridden before. One morning Sergeant Pettit took the lot of us out to show us how it was done.

We saddled up, took our horses from the picket ropes, and led them into a field, where we stood in a row, each man by his horse. The sergeant was out in front facing us.

He had a series of orders for us, and showed us what happened on each one.

First, we "stood to horse." That meant standing erect, just as we did when we were told to assume the "position of a soldier," except that each man held his horse's reins in his right hand just twelve inches from the bit.

The next order was "prepare to mount," and all we did was pivot on the heel and swing around in a right face.

Then came the order to "mount," and the way Pettit did it, it looked very easy; it was just as if he floated up into the saddle. As a matter of fact, it wasn't really so hard to do, once you learned the trick of getting your left toe into the stirrup, resting one hand on the pommel of the saddle, and giving an easy little spring with the right foot.

But some of the boys had trouble—you'd be surprised how many gave too much of a spring and went right on over the horse to take a header on the other side—and Joss spent the whole morning with us. He made us do it over and over, and he had lots of words of advice. . . . "Don't put your arm around his neck—you aren't supposed to wrastle with him, all you want to do is just get in the saddle," and so on.

Then, of course, came the actual riding. Here I had a little surprise. For some reason it came easy to me.

Lots of the boys were scared to death once they got up in the saddle. With the help of Joss Pettit they got on, but they weren't a bit sure they could stay on, and the ground looked an awful long way down. I noticed a lot of great big lummoxes, a head taller than I was, who would sit all crunched up, white around the lips, hardly daring to roll their eyes for fear they'd take a tumble; yet somehow I seemed to feel at home there. Perhaps it was because Red and I were such good friends that it seemed natural to be up on his back. Perhaps it was because, on a horse, I could forget I was shorter than most of the rest and feel as big and husky as anybody. Whatever it was, I didn't have very much trouble learning to ride. When I got into the saddle I felt as if I belonged there.

That certainly wasn't the way with everybody. When we started trotting around the field, there were a lot of tumbles. We were just doing an easy trot, so nobody really hurt himself, but after each spill the sergeant had something to say. Of course the ones who hadn't fallen would laugh and I would feel real proud of myself.

But I might have known that Sergeant Pettit would have fixed ideas on how you ought to ride. It wasn't nearly enough just to stay on your horse; while you stayed on you had to look the way Joss Pettit thought you ought to look, and he could sure make a commotion if you weren't doing it to suit him.

Just as I was kind of patting myself on the back because it seemed easier for me than for most of the rest, Sergeant Pettit was yelling at me to keep my elbows in, and was asking me if I thought I was a bird flapping my wings. A minute later he'd ride over close and snap out to me that one hand was enough for the reins, and did I think maybe I ought to have a railing around me, or a groom to hold me in the saddle so I wouldn't fall; then he'd get into a regular tantrum about troopers who rode all hunched over and couldn't sit up straight.

Now that I think of it, "tantrum" isn't really the word. When he was mad, which was quite often, Sergeant Pettit held very still and made no unnecessary moves. It was just his voice that got out of line.

What made him maddest of all was to have somebody hold onto the pommel of the saddle while he rode.

"Leggo that leather!" he would shout. "Your saddle is to sit in, not to hold onto. Leggo, I tell you!"

By the end of the day we were all winded, and I began to think I never would be able to satisfy Sergeant Pettit. Before we went back to the stables he looked us over, very disgusted. He drew a deep breath, and I expected him to swear and storm really hard. Instead he let his breath out, real slow, in a long sigh, and when he spoke his voice was flat and kind of tired-sounding.

"You sure don't look like troopers," he said. Then his face brightened, and he smiled a grim little smile. When he spoke the old rasp was back in his voice.

"You will, though, before I'm done with you!" he promised.

He was as good as his word. He gave us between eight and ten hours of his attention every day for weeks, and finally we were ready to be assigned to regular companies. Then we began to feel more like soldiers; also, we learned how a cavalry regiment is put together.

The regiment had twelve companies, or troops. Each troop was supposed to contain one hundred men, although it was only at the start that we ever had that many. Inside of six months, what with men getting sick, going on special details or just plain drifting away, we were down to where most companies didn't average more than fifty men apiece.

Two companies made a squadron, and two squadrons

made a battalion. There were three battalions in the regiment, each commanded by a major. Sergeant Pettit said that out in the Indian country, before the war, the battalions used to operate separately. The way it worked with us, though, the regiment stayed in one piece, and in the end the battalion organization was more or less forgotten.

I got into B Troop. Otis was in K, so we weren't thrown together much. Most of the men in B came from the central part of the state, and there wasn't anybody in it that I knew or that even came from any town I'd ever been in. When the whole regiment lined up on parade, B Company was always at the left end of the line. Company A was at the right end, the post of honor, but B's place was the second post of honor and we were very proud of it.

One thing I liked, although I didn't expect to like it. When we got organized, Sergeant Pettit was in B Company. I had begun by being scared to death of that little man. Then I had hated him. Now I was beginning to see that it was good to have him around.

Sergeant Pettit was regular army—he'd done a couple of hitches, fighting Indians, before the war—and he was very hard-boiled. Just as he had warned us, when he told us to do something we had to jump, and no back talk. But he always knew what he was about. I could see that the way to be a good soldier was to watch him, listen to him, and do everything just the way he said to do it.

More than anything else I wanted to be a good soldier. I'd run away from Pine Bay, really, because I felt too undersized and repressed ever to measure up in that roughneck little lumber town. But Sergeant Pettit was no bigger than I was, yet he could have made Pine Bay and everybody in it jump through a hoop. I wanted to be like him.

I don't mean that I wanted to be spit-in-your-eye tough, the way he was; but I was beginning to understand that before you could be tough with the rest of the world, you had to be tough with yourself. You had to be tough with all of the things you yourself were afraid of. What made skinny little Joss Pettit so strong was the fact that he wasn't afraid of a thing. Under everything else, he had a don't-give-a-damn streak. That was why he was always ready to shoot the works. He had licked something down inside, so he could lick things on the outside, too, or if they licked him it didn't really matter.

We got our carbines about this time. We were in luck, because we got Colt's revolving rifles. They were little short sawed-off-looking carbines, seven-shot repeaters, with a cylinder just like a revolver's in the breech. Most cavalry regiments then drew single-shooters. As a result, we could shoot rings around most other outfits, either Yanks or Rebels.

In addition we drew revolvers, and Sergeant Pettit told us we belonged to one of the best-equipped regiments in the whole army.

"Don't ever let 'em take this away from you," he said, patting his own revolver. "In a charge, now, with a line of Rebel troopers coming at you, you're a hundred times better off with this hand gun than with your saber. You can pop the other fellow out of his saddle before he gets close enough to swing at you, and——"

I lost the rest of what he was saying, because for the first time I realized that at the end of all of this equipping and drilling and so on there was going to be some fighting with real live enemies. I felt something cold in my chest, like a lump of ice; it seemed as if I could see a line of big men galloping at me, yelling and swinging their sabers, and right there I knew that under everything else I was an awful coward. I hoped our stay in training camp would last forever. I just wasn't up to a battle. I didn't have the nerve, and I'd known from the start that I didn't have it: so what in the world was I going to do? I could pretend I was brave, for a while—but wouldn't Joss Pettit surely find me out? Then wouldn't his terrible scorn be even worse than anything the Rebs could do to me?

We drew sabers, too, at last, which I thought were nice to have, even if Sergeant Pettit did have such a low opinion of them. Wearing one made me feel like a soldier the way nothing else did.

They came in metal scabbards, and saber and scabbard together were fairly heavy. The iron rings on the scabbard to which the carrying straps were fastened jingled against the metal when your horse trotted. I thought it made a pleasant sound, that little irregular jingling, as a column of men trotted along, but the sergeant said it was very bad.

"Lets everybody within half a mile know you're riding by," he said. "How you going to ride past a camp full of braves—I mean Rebels—at night without their knowing it? Might as well send up rockets and be done with it."

The straps that fastened the scabbard to your waist belt were long, so that when you were mounted the grip of the saber lay handy about halfway up your left thigh and you could draw the blade easily. On foot, though, the lower end of the scabbard dragged on the ground, so the thing to do then was hook it up—put the topmost ring of the scabbard on a little hook at the left side of your belt. It was hard to draw the saber, hooked up, but it didn't bump along the ground. Still, there was something sort of negligent and elegant looking, the way a real cavalryman could stroll around trailing his scabbard, and most of us tried it that way—which disgusted our sergeant.

"Leave the things lay under the forage rack—that's the best place for 'em anyhow!" he said.

Sometimes it seemed as if Sergeant Pettit wasn't happy except when he was grumbling.

6. WE'VE GOT TO BE TOUGH

It was along in November before we finally left camp. It had begun to seem as if we would stay there forever, and a lot of the boys began to complain that the war was likely to end before we got into it. Sergeant Pettit said we shouldn't worry; the war was going to go on for a long time, and each and every one of us would get a regular bellyful of it before it was finished. Anyway, we weren't fit for field service yet. By rights they ought to keep us in camp for a solid year, if not for two, because there was lots more to being a trooper than just learning how to sit on a horse.

"Not that most of you backwoodsmen have even learned how to do that yet," he added contemptuously.

Late in October we had been formally mustered into Federal service. Until then we had actually been state troops. Now we were, officially, the second regiment of Michigan Cavalry, United States Volunteers. It made the war seem nearer and soldiering more real. That night I got a pencil and a tablet and sat down in my tent to write a long letter to Uncle Ebenezer, telling him just what I had done and where I was.

I don't think I really expected to get an answer; I had disobeyed him, I had deceived him, and I halfway thought he was going to disown me forever. But in less than a week I had a letter from him, in the angular, stiff, hard-fisted script I had seen so often on his ledgers, and it was a very nice letter. It said:

My dear nephew: I was glad to get your letter. I have worried much about you and I am greatly relieved to learn that you are well. It was wrong of you, of course, to run off without my permission. It would have been better had you at least waited until your eighteenth birthday, when in a manner of speaking you would have been reaching man's estate. But what is done is done, and my prayer now is that you may be spared amid the uncertainties of this terrible war and may some day return to us. Beware of temptation and loose living, remember now thy Creator in the days of thy youth, and commit yourself always to the keeping of Him without Whose knowledge not even a sparrow falls. Write to me when your duties give you leisure.

Affectionately,
Uncle Ebenezer

This really floored me. For Uncle Ebenezer, it was practically gushing. It even made me wonder: Would it have been better, perhaps, if I had not run off the way I did but had simply faced up to him and told him that I was going? I worried some about that. Anyway, it was nice to know that I really did have a home after all, even though I probably wasn't going to see it for a long time. I felt as if I had something to tie to. I never was a very good correspondent, but after that I wrote to Uncle Ebenezer as often as I could get around to it.

Shortly after this our regiment got its marching orders. We were bound for St. Louis. Most of the trip would be by train, and we quickly discovered that moving a full cavalry regiment involves a terrible lot of hard work.

Our training camp was situated in what was ordinarily the state fairgrounds. There were railroad sidings at the far end of the place, so we didn't have to go parading through the city to get on the cars, which was just as well, because loading up was pretty involved.

There was a long train of passenger cars to carry us soldiers, and we got our belongings stowed away without much trouble. Then we saw three trains of freight cars, with around thirty-five or forty cars in each train, drawn up for our horses. Getting all of those animals aboard was a job. What we called our horse furniture—saddles, bridles, and so on—had to be packed away in boxcars, and other cars had to be filled with hay and straw for the horses, so that, altogether, it took the better part of twenty-four hours before everything was loaded and our little fleet of trains pulled out.

We went to Detroit first, where we had to unload our horses, ourselves, and everything else and transfer to another set of trains. Then we went puffing off across southern Michigan, and at every city and town there were crowds down at the station to wave to us and cheer. Sometimes when the train stopped they'd bring big wash baskets full of sandwiches and great big pots of coffee and pass them into our cars.

Once every twenty-four hours we had to pull up somewhere, take our horses out of their cars, and give them food and water, while details cleaned the cars and laid down fresh straw. This was too much like hard work to be much fun, and one day, at some stop in Illinois, somebody complained that the army took better care of the horses than it did of the men.

"Of course it does," said Sergeant Pettit. "We can get recruits anywhere, but these horses cost money."

It must have been nearly a week later that we got to Alton, Illinois, where we moved horses and baggage to a couple of river steamers, and that night we went cruising down the Mississippi. Next morning we were in St. Louis, and after we unloaded we saddled up and rode out to Benton Barracks, which, said Sergeant Pettit, was where the army was going to take the rough edges off of us.

Benton Barracks was a big place. The sergeant said it was the army's main cavalry depot (he pronounced it "deppo") and, when we got a look at it, that far-off fairgrounds camp at Grand Rapids began to seem awfully small and makeshift.

We came in through the main gate, passed a brick guardhouse and offices, and rode out across an enormous parade ground; it was at least a mile long and a quarter of a mile wide, flat as a floor, with barracks on three sides of it. The barracks were two stories high, of brick, with white verandas running all across the front. They looked old and solid, as if the army had been here for a long time and was going to go on being here for a long time, secession or no.

The dead grass on the parade ground was worn off and beaten down. It occurred to me that a lot of cavalry must have done a great deal of drilling to put it in that shape. I figured that before we got away we were probably going to contribute to that treatment.

Over beyond the barracks were cook sheds, blacksmith huts, wheelwrights' shops, forage sheds, and what looked like miles and miles of stables, with long rows of army wagons parked beyond. Everything was neat and orderly and under control, yet there was always a sense of noise and movement in the air—the sound of marching columns on the parade ground, the jingle-jangle of equipments, the clank and clang from the smithies and the shops, muffled bugle calls from beyond the barracks, shouted commands from far off, as if a great many men were busy doing a great many different things. The army seemed immense. For the first time I had a feeling of being part of something much bigger than I had ever imagined before. I began to understand how big and great and everlasting the United States really was.

We spent most of four months at Benton Barracks, and the time raced by. The reason, I suppose, was that we were kept so busy. As the sergeant said, here was where the army took our rough edges off, and it bore down hard while it was doing it. Those days there just was no way to please Joss Pettit.

When I try to remember that time I can only seem to recall a few separate incidents. All the rest seems to be the same thing—endless hours of mounted drill, the drumming of horses' hoofs, the everlasting notes of the bugle, the barking cries of the officers, the smell of sweat and leather and dust and stables, the band playing at evening parade with the sunset gun going Bump! with a noise that jarred the eardrums, and the flag sliding down the tall pole, with endless lines of mounted men at attention on the dusty-brown field . . . the same thing day after day and week after week, the regiment slowly but surely growing harder and more compact, each individual soldier doing exactly the same thing. Yes, they did take the rough edges off.

The biggest single thing that happened to us was that we got a new colonel. Lieutenant Colonel Davies left us. He was just too old to stand the grind, and one morning we saw a stocky, black-headed man with a bald forehead and a bushy beard ride out to take charge of us, Colonel Gordon Granger.

Granger was a regular, a rough, tough customer to boot, with a voice you could hear halfway to Chattanooga. He could take one look at the regiment riding by in column of squadrons and see a cinch strap buckled wrong at the far end of the second rank of the third squadron. Then he would call out about it so that everybody in the regiment knew just who the culprit was. He kept us on the parade ground everlastingly; we had such a lot to learn, and if we didn't learn about it before spring it was not going to be for want of lessons.

As we worked at it, I began to see that a thousand of the best riders in the world wouldn't make a cavalry *regiment* without drill. The regiment had to have a life of its own. It had to be trained so that the colonel could do anything with it just by speaking a few words of command— steer it to right or left, make it change its shape, swing it

69

out in a great sweeping arc with a thousand mounted men cutting across the field like the blade of an enormous scythe, break it into groups and send the groups off in a moving pattern of their own, then bring them all back together into a compact mass. . . . This sort of thing was necessary, not just for parade ground show, but so that the regiment could do the work it would have to do when it got out on active service.

So we put in hour after hour, day after day, learning how to go from a single-rank company front into a column of fours, how to swing from that into troop or squadron front, how to form a battalion front from column, how to do it at a walk or a trot or a dead gallop. We had to learn how to do it all by bugle calls, instead of by word-of-mouth orders. (You could always hear the bugles, but with eight hundred or a thousand men galloping and yelling the chances were you couldn't hear a spoken command.)

We had to be able to do all of these things (and a dozen more which I haven't mentioned) when it was dark, or where the ground was rough or the country was all cut up with bushes and stumps and trees; and we had to do all of these things so many times that at last they became second nature and we could do them without thinking about how they were done.

Last but not least, our horses had to learn all of these things, too. I was surprised to find out that Red and most of the other horses could recognize the bugle calls and knew what to do when they heard them. They knew their places in line, too, and they got it into their heads that they belonged in those places and they didn't want to leave them. Once in a while, if a man fell off his horse while we were drilling, we'd notice that his horse would stay in position and go on with the rest of the troop, doing whatever maneuver was called for; although at other times, if a man lost his seat, his horse would stop and wait for him, and if he was flat on the ground it would even nuzzle him as if it wanted to help.

Not all of our drilling was done on the parade ground. Colonel Granger liked to take us out in the open country and put us through our paces on ground that was more like what we'd see when we got out on active service. One of his favorite tricks was to take the regiment cross-country at a good swinging trot, and get it up to the lip of some ravine or deep hollow—usually a place with boulders or fallen trees or other obstacles. Then he would turn in his saddle and call out, in that tremendous voice: "Here's where the infantry can get off and walk, but by thunder the *cavalry* is going to ride!"

Then over the brink he would go, and the regiment after him, all of us yelling, most of us scared half to death. I was really awfully frightened, but I was beginning to find that if you try hard enough you can at least keep your fear down out of sight where nobody else can see it—and if you do, somehow, it isn't quite so powerful.

We didn't like Colonel Granger at first. He was too hard, too demanding, too much regular army in his attitude. The routine under Colonel Davies seemed very easygoing by contrast, when we looked back on it, and we didn't care much for the change. But after a while we began to be proud of the stiff training and discipline we were getting, and when we learned that the colonel was proud of us—well, that settled it. From then on we thought he was great.

We discovered that he was proud of us one afternoon when we were coming in through the main gate after a long ride in the open country. Dusty and tired, we were coming along in column of fours, thinking about nothing much except how nice it was going to be to dismount and make the horses comfortable and have some supper. Colonel Granger had been at the head of the column, but he reined in after he went through the gate and sat there, watching us pass. As my company went by we saw him turn and call to another officer who was just coming out of the headquarters offices.

"Pope, look at that!" Granger called, gesturing toward the moving column. The other officer looked and shrugged.

"Well, what of it?" he asked.

Granger looked angry.

"What of it, you idiot?" he cried. "Did you ever see such a good-looking, well-drilled regiment in all your life?"

That did it. Without realizing it, we wanted that tough colonel of ours to think well of us. Now we had heard him say that he was actually proud of us. We were proud of ourselves after that, and we figured we were the best cavalry regiment in the whole army—or would be, anyway, as soon as we had met the Rebels a couple of times.

One other thing I remember from those days was a fight I had. It wasn't much of a fight, as such things go, but in an indirect way it had some important results—important for me, that is.

It happened one afternoon in early February when my

platoon was sent out to escort a dozen wagons that were bringing in some forage. We were down at a farm where the wagons were being loaded, our horses picketed to some trees, and we'd built little fires and were boiling some coffee.

There was a big, sleepy Dutchman in our platoon named Gus Heinz, who was all hands and feet. If there was a way to be extra clumsy about anything, Gus would find it. So pretty soon he went blobbing past where I was sitting, and stepped on the end of a stick that was in my fire. When he did, the other end of the stick flew up and spilled my can of coffee. I jumped up and called him a big-footed Dutch ox. He called me an underfed west Michigan lumber camp scalawag, and first thing anybody knew we were going at it with our fists.

Gus was a lot bigger and I ought to have had a bad licking. I got a bloody nose first thing, and was on my way to get a good deal worse, when Gus's foot slipped and he went off balance. Just as he did, I hit him, and since he was off balance anyway he fell down. I flung myself on him as he rolled over to get up, figuring I would pound his head in the dirt—in the scraps we used to have when I was a kid, that was the way to make the other fellow holler "Enough!"

But Gus was very clumsy, and I guess I was pretty clumsy myself. When I jumped on him my knee accidentally hit him in the pit of the stomach and he doubled up, turned green, and couldn't get his breath. It turned out I had won the fight . . . such as it was.

After Gus got straightened out, I went down to a little

brook to wash the blood off my face. When I got through and started back, there was Joss Pettit, watching me.

"That was a ragged fight," he said. "What did you want to slug with a big farmer like that for, anyhow?"

"I got mad," I said.

"I could see that," said Joss. "I mean, why fist-fight with him? You shoulda grappled with him right away."

I looked blank, and he went on to explain.

"You aren't big enough to use your fists much," he said. "You're like me, that way. People like us, when we fight, we got to get in close. Those other people got longer arms. They push our noses in and knock our teeth out if we try to fist-fight. We got to make a wrastle out of it, quick. That way we can butt, or gouge, or give 'em the knee—like you finally did. Only I don't think you meant to do it."

"I didn't," I admitted. I was feeling good because Joss had said I was like him. Up to now he'd always acted as if I was a worm in the dust.

"'Tisn't really fair, though, to butt and gouge and use knees, is it?" I asked him.

Joss looked at me with contempt.

"Fair?" he said. "What's 'fair' got to do with it? You get in a fight with a man, you got to hurt him before he hurts you. You don't care anything about being fair. What you care about is winning the fight."

I wasn't quite satisfied and I guess my face showed it, for Joss went on with the argument.

"If you're just sparring with a friend, that's different," he said. "We're talking about fighting. The great big fellows can afford to worry about being fair. Us little fellows can't. We got to be tough. You remember that. Hurt the other fellow before he hurts you, and do it any way you can. If it's a real serious fight, hurt him as bad as you know how. And do it quick, because if you don't you'll get it yourself."

It used to strike me, afterward, that what the sergeant said was pretty good advice for armies as well as for individual soldiers. The men who won battles in that war seemed to operate pretty much along Joss Pettit's line.

But what was important to me was that somehow that fight, and the little word of advice he gave me, seemed to stick in the sergeant's mind. He began to notice me. I suppose he thought I had a little spunk and he liked spunk. Anyway, about that time Corporal Ernie Nofsinger of our squad got the measles. When he was getting over the measles something went wrong with his hearing, so the surgeon finally certified him for a medical discharge. They called me in and made me a corporal in his place, which meant I got two big yellow chevrons to wear on my sleeves and a couple dollars more a month in my pay. I think it was Joss Pettit who was responsible for it, although I never dared ask him about it.

7. WE WISHED WE'D STAYED AT HOME

At the end of February we left Benton Barracks and went off to war. They loaded us on big river steamers and we went downstream to a little bit of a town called Commerce. There we unloaded and saddled up to ride cross-country to join the army of General John Pope, who was trying to capture a Rebel stronghold at New Madrid.

That cross-country march was one of the worst I made in all the war. It seemed as if there was some sort of omen in it because we didn't have any good luck for months afterward.

It was nearly dark when we started. It had been drizzling rain, and the weather was chilly. The river had been rising so that the country we were crossing had turned into a regular swamp, with dank-looking tree trunks coming up out of pools of black, ugly water, and all the little shacks on the farms and in the miserable little villages looked discouraged and kind of no-account, as if the people who lived in them were never going to amount to anything and knew it, and had long since stopped caring about it.

We Wished We'd Stayed at Home

The road wound off past a few farms and went into a bleak woodland. It was deep with soupy mud that got worse and worse as the horses plodded on. Night came down, and the drizzle turned into a mean, pelting rain. We got soaking wet. The long column moved at a crawl, mud squelching underfoot, everybody chilly and miserable, and the march kept on all night long.

Once or twice we halted for a breather. There was plenty of wood all around us, but it was too wet to build fires, so we couldn't make coffee as we usually did at such times. When we dismounted we stood in mud halfway to our knees—Big Red making unhappy noises 'way down in his throat—and when we remounted our pants were wet and our saddles were wet. Any ideas I ever had about how romantic it was to be in the cavalry went away right then and never came back.

There were Rebs loose in this country. An Indiana cavalry regiment which was on the road in front of us ran into some Reb outpost during the night. Our column halted in the pitch darkness. Up ahead somewhere we could hear scattering shots as the Indiana boys moved in on the Rebs. It was an eerie, discomforting sound, that firing in the wet night. We couldn't tell what was going on, and for a while we thought we might get into the fight, too, so we loosened our carbines in the leather boots that held them on the right side of the saddles. But then the firing stopped, our bugles sounded—they had a weird, nerve-racking sound, in the black, wet air, that hurt the ears somehow—and then we were in the saddle, riding on again.

Once, in the dark, we passed a little group huddled in

the underbrush, and some man was moaning: "Oh my God! Oh my God!" over and over, as if he couldn't stop. It sounded awful. I'd known, of course, that men got hurt in battles, but this sounded close and intimate and real, not like something you read about in the papers. Anyhow there really hadn't been a battle—just some men shooting at each other in a freezing rain at midnight. I began to imagine what it would be like to be hurt so bad you'd make a noise like the one I'd just heard. For a few minutes it didn't seem as if I could ever possibly make myself go into a real battle. I found myself wishing that I was back in Michigan watching the schooners coming in from the big lake, with a carpet of logs on the surface of the river back above the mill, and lazy white clouds drifting across an empty blue sky.

The night ended finally, but daylight didn't seem to help much. It was still raining; not very hard, but persistently, as if there wasn't anything that could ever stop it. The country looked half drowned, and the men in our column looked most nearly drowned of all. We came up to the outposts of General Pope's army after a while, and after another long and uncomfortable halt by the roadside we went on through the infantry camps.

Pope's men had pup tents. There seemed to be acres and acres of these pitched in the fields, all of them looking as if the water would rise and float them away pretty soon if they didn't sink out of sight in the mud first. There was a smudge in the air from the breakfast fires the infantry had built, and all the soldiers we saw looked as if they had been plastered with mud weeks ago and had never bothered to try to get any of it off.

We turned into a big field, laid out picket ropes, un-saddled, and did the best we could to make our horses comfortable. Our wagon train was lost back in the rear some place, so there wasn't any forage. We got grain from our saddlebags and the horses ate. When they had been taken care of we went to work to do something for ourselves.

There was not very much we could do. The army had not issued pup tents to our regiment, so when we left Benton Barracks we had put the big Sibley tents in our wagons. These tents were very fine things. Each one was circular, rising to a high peak in the center, and a dozen men could sleep comfortably in one tent. We usually lay with our feet toward the center, spread out around the center pole like the spokes of a wheel. When there was a little straw to put on the ground, a Sibley tent was as good as a house.

The trouble was that all of these fine tents were in the wagons and the wagons were stuck in the mud twenty miles away. It would be days before we saw them again. Meanwhile, we had no tents, no straw, no shelter of any kind, and making a camp was simply a matter of flopping down in the mud. The field we were in had been plowed the autumn before, and there was no sod; just mud, getting deeper and stickier by the minute.

We sent details to get firewood and we did our best to cook breakfast, but our best was not very good. We finally got fires built but they were mostly smoke, which burned our eyes and made us cough. When we tried to frizzle slices of salt pork they just got soggy and a little charred around the edges, but we ate them anyhow—we were hungry enough to eat anything—and we ate hardtack, and drank the miserable excuse for coffee that we had boiled over those miserable excuses for campfires. Then we laid our rubber blankets in the mud, sprawled on top of them, pulled our wet blankets up under our chins, and tried to get some sleep.

I thought this was the worst experience a soldier could have (although I was not much older before I realized that in a lot of ways it was just about average) and I was certain that I would catch an awful cold and die of pneumonia. I felt very sorry for myself. None of the things I'd set out to do when I ran away to enlist seemed to matter. I didn't care who won the war, or whether I was a hero or a coward, or whether Joss Pettit ever came to like me; I just knew I was going to die in the cold and wet. I would have worried and pitied myself into a dreadful state except that I dropped off to sleep and slept for hours, with the rain coming down on my face.

Somehow I didn't catch cold at all. When I finally pulled myself out of those soggy blankets and did the little I could to dry myself and get a bit of the mud off, I was stiff, sore, hungry, and mad at all the world, but outside of that I was actually feeling good. It flabbergasted me. I'd always been delicate. If I got my feet wet or sat in a draft, I'd be sick for days. But what I'd just been through hadn't hurt me at all.

On the stable line that morning I worked up nerve enough to mention this to Joss Pettit. He told me that wiry, undersized little men were really a lot tougher than the big husky ones, and a good cavalry regiment ought to have nothing but little men in it. It was the big ones, he said, who caught cold or got camp diarrhea or came down with measles or typhoid or mumps, and wound up in hospital or were laid away under the ground. The frail, skinny-looking youngsters were the ones who turned out to be the best troopers.

What Joss said did me more good than a warm bed and a white-fish dinner. I kept my eyes open, the next few days, and began to see that there was a lot in what he said. That camp in the rain thinned our regiment out something awful. So many men caught cold and got pneumonia that I think that night march and the bivouac in the mud cost the regiment more men than a hard battle would have done. It did seem to be the big men who got hit the worst. I remember how A and E companies, full of strapping huskies from the lumber camps around Saginaw and Muskegon, came down almost to skeleton strength. Our own company, which had a lot of town fellows from Grand Rapids who had looked pasty and hollow-chested when they enlisted, made out a lot better. For the first time I began to be glad I was just the size I was.

Anyway, most of us did live through it, even if we never again had as many as eight hundred men present for duty in a regiment which was twelve hundred strong when it left Grand Rapids. Our wagons came up in a couple of days, and when we got our tents we figured things would be better. But the whole country was like a swamp. We never could really get any of our clothing more than half dry, and getting ourselves clean was entirely out of the question.

Then, to make matters worse, we lost Colonel Granger. What happened was that Colonel Granger was pro-

moted brigadier general and put in charge of a whole
brigade. That was fine, except that he stopped being our
colonel, and after he left nothing seemed to go right. Major Gorham, who had been in charge of the second battalion, took command of the regiment. He was a good man
and had fought at Bull Run with some three-months regiment, but he was not a regular and he just didn't know
what Colonel Granger knew about taking care of a regiment.

We could see the difference. We seemed to march away
from our wagons oftener than before. More and more
there would be some mix-up that kept forage for our
horses from coming up; or when we went to draw rations
we'd find the commissary had nothing but hardtack, and
we'd live on dry crackers for a few days. We moved
around a good bit in those days, scouting around the
flanks of Pope's army, and on the march our regiment
didn't seem to be well organized. We would saddle up,
then stand to horse for a couple of hours before we began
to move. When a march began it would go by fits and
starts—long, meaningless halts, frantic hurry in between
the halts, orders to move coming in just when we had
boiled coffee and fried bacon and were getting ready to
eat dinner, rest at night broken by some senseless order to
move camp a couple of miles just after everybody had
gone to sleep.

This might not have been so bad—although it wore out
men and horses, and our regiment kept on shrinking—except that we didn't seem to be accomplishing anything in
particular. There was a lot of firing going on along the
infantry lines, and day after day we could hear volleys of

musketry and the heavy, bumping thud of artillery fire; yet we always seemed to be off on the fringes of it, prowling around in empty country outside the firing zone. We were glad enough that we were not getting hurt, of course, but there didn't seem any good reason why we might not just as well be back in recruit camp, because nothing we were doing now seemed necessary or important.

We could see the infantry felt that way about us, too. When we rode past a line of infantry we were sure to hear nasty remarks. Some infantryman would call out to another, real loud, for our benefit:

"Jim! You seen any dead cavalrymen lately?"

And Jim would guffaw and say: "*Dead* cavalrymen? Don't be a big fool. *Nobody* ever saw a dead cavalryman."

Now and then, of course, things would be so that some of the boys could work up a fist fight about it, which would help a little. But we couldn't help remembering that a big siege was going on, with infantry and artillery under fire, losing men to Rebel bullets every day, while nobody in our regiment had been hit because our regiment never really got into any action.

Once in a while we'd flush a Reb cavalry patrol out on the roads somewhere, and go galloping along for a mile or two, Rebs and Yanks firing from the saddle, making a big racket but hardly ever hitting anybody. Now and then we'd be placed where an occasional Rebel shell would go flying overhead, and if it made any difference to anybody we could at least say we had been under fire. Still, there it was—we weren't really doing any fighting. The men who were fighting resented it and let us know that they resented it, and there wasn't very much we could say about it.

Looking back, it seems as if this went on for a long time. Actually, it only lasted about a month. Early in April we got news that over in Tennessee there had been a tremendous battle at a place called Shiloh and that our side had won. About that time the Rebs at New Madrid caved in and the Mississippi was open all the way down to Memphis. Then one day our regiment, along with many others, marched down to the river to board steamboats again; and a big fleet of river boats with a couple of black, squat-looking gunboats leading the way went for a long cruise.

We went up the river all the way to Cairo, turned up the Ohio, and finally went up the Tennessee. We were out of the mud and the drowned-looking river country, and the sight of hills and green forests and cultivated farms made us feel better. We disembarked at a place called Hamburg Landing, which was so far down in Tennessee that it was almost over the line in Mississippi. From there we began marching west and south to join up with General Halleck's army.

This army, we found out, was almighty big—close to one hundred and twenty thousand men in it, counting everybody—and it was moving down to chase the Rebs out of a railway junction town called Corinth, in Mississippi. Halleck's army had three "wings"; one under General U. S. Grant, another under General Don Carlos Buell, and the third under our old Mississippi river acquaintance General Pope, who had come across overland while we were taking our long river trip.

We Wished We'd Stayed at Home

We were still part of Pope's force, so we went trotting on down into the state of Mississippi trying to overtake him. As we went we were reminded that life in the army has a way of going to extremes. If you escape from one thing that's bad, you generally get its exact opposite, usually equally bad in a different way.

We had been wallowing in the mud and water for so long that we used to say if we could just get where it was dry we would never complain again. Well, where we were now it was dry—terribly dry, with dust in the roads six inches deep, powdery dust like flour that floated up and filled the air whenever a column of troops moved, so that we got dust under our clothing, in our hair, ears, eyes, and mouth, and all over everything, making our blue uniforms look exactly like Rebel gray.

We moved in the center of a choking cloud of dust that covered leaves and branches clear to the tops of the trees. Unless you were somewhere outside of the moving column you couldn't see thirty feet. The water in your canteen would all be gone before you had been on the march two hours—or, if you did save a little, it would get warm and kind of sickish, and when you finally drank some the dust in your mouth would turn to mud and gag you.

The weather was very hot and there were not very many streams. We had thought we were dirty, back in camp at New Madrid, but now we could see that we hadn't known the first thing about how dirty men can get. We realized that while rain and mud were bad, for all-around discomfort and misery heat and dust were ever so much worse.

The campaigning we were doing here didn't raise our spirits any, either. The Union army was moving very slowly. The Rebs were drawing back as we came on—drawing back deliberately, as if they hated to, putting up a sharp little fight every now and then from some ridge or tangled wood. As we advanced the cavalry would go on ahead, to make the Rebs in these places show themselves. We would dismount and skirmish on foot until the Rebel position was clear; then we'd remount and go to the rear, and the infantry would come up to drive the Rebels out.

That's the way all armies do it, but it didn't improve our standing with the infantry to speak of. When we would go riding back to the rear, infantrymen would see us and holler to each other: "Must be going to be a fight—I see the cavalry is going to the rear."

Once we came out of a mean little pasture by a dry creek bed, full of brambles and stumps and fallen logs. Anybody could see it was just the sort of place where a few determined Johnnies could hang on and give their attackers a bad time of it. We rode back through the ranks of an infantry skirmish line that was going up into all of this. The infantry looked tense and thin-lipped because they knew what they were getting into and, as we passed, one foot soldier looked up at me and snarled:

"That's right—get back to the rear and give a *man* a chance!"

I don't know that I ever felt much lower than I did right then. I forgot how scared I was when I heard the guns going off, and actually wished we could get into a great big fight. Anything, I thought—anything at all, no matter how bad it is—would be better than having a fighting man look at you that way and show his contempt for you.

April had gone, and most of May, as we moved slowly

down into Mississippi. We were dirty and tired, and being in the cavalry seemed the worst thing that could happen to a soldier. Some of the men deserted, and we never saw them again, and there were times when all of us felt a little like doing the same thing. We began to wish that we had joined some other branch of the service, or even that we hadn't joined anything at all and had stayed home, like sensible people. The weather was bad, the rations were worse, and we were sorry we ever got mixed up in this war.

And then we met Phil Sheridan.

★

8. SHERIDAN'S WAY

We got him unexpectedly. Rumors about a new colonel
had been making the rounds, but by now we let rumors
go in one ear and out the other because we weren't really
expecting anything. It was close to the end of May. We
were in the army lines near Corinth, when orders came
through that our regiment and the 2d Iowa were to go east
and break a Rebel railway line at a place called Booneville.

We were supposed to set out after dark, so at sundown
we were busy getting ready—putting rations and forage
in the sadddlebags, getting blankets and rubber ponchos
rolled up and strapped at the rear of the saddle, making
sure our revolvers and carbine ammunition was in the
proper place, and so on—when Sheridan came riding into
camp.

There wasn't anything impressive about him. He was a
little, rather awkward-looking Irishman with a black
head and a dark skin, a colonel's eagles stitched on the
shoulders of what had been a captain's uniform. We saw
him shaking hands with Major Gorham and the other

officers, with the dusk coming down. Then somebody was holding a lantern while he studied a map, and he was nodding and saying: "All right! All right!" Then the bugles sounded, and in another moment the regiment was jogging down the road in column of fours, the new colonel in the lead.

In some ways it was like any other assignment, and in other ways it was a little different.

It was a hot, windless night, and the road led through woods with the treetops meeting overhead, so it was like riding down a dark tunnel full of dust. We went clumping along, hot and sticky, not paying much attention to anything. After about an hour the road came out into open country, climbed a hill, and went along the top of a ridge. There was some air stirring here and it felt a good deal cooler.

We expected to be ordered to trot. That was the way those night marches always went. Where the going was bad the regiment walked, and when things got better it would speed up. When the horses began to get winded it would come down to a walk again, and after five minutes there would be another trot. The column would string out along the road, the head of it always moving a little faster than the tail, while the road behind it would be cluttered with men whose horses had broken down, or with stragglers who were hanging back to take it easy. After a while there'd be a halt for an hour to let everybody catch up.

But this time we got a different order. Back from the head of the column came the word for everybody to dismount and walk, leading his horse.

Our regiment was moving that night in a way they called "left in front." That is, the head of the column would have been the left end of the regiment if the whole outfit had been lined up in a double rank on the parade ground; this meant that the company I was in, Company B, was at the head of the column. Now that we were out of the woods, we could see a little in the gray starlight, and Sheridan himself was only a few yards ahead of where I was riding; when he passed the word for everybody to dismount he got off his own horse, too, and walked along like everybody else, reins in his right hand.

That was all right, and I didn't think much about it, one way or the other. We walked for about an hour, I suppose, then Sheridan said something to his bugler, swung up into the saddle, and the order to mount floated down the air. But still we did not get any orders to trot, and by-and-by it dawned on me that we were going to move at this pace all night.

Some time after midnight we halted for ten minutes. When we did, I saw Sheridan and another officer go cantering back along the column, and when he had returned to the head of it we started on again. After a while the sky ahead of us began to get lighter, so that we could make out the hills and woods in the distance. There was a thin mist lying close to the ground, and somewhere round about us the birds began to wake up and call to one another in an experimental sort of way. We had ridden all night, and off somewhere we could hear a train whistle, lonely and mournful, as if the countryside was haunted. The column came to a halt, and Sheridan went trotting up to the top of a little hillock at the right of the road.

Behind us the road was in view for a mile or so, and I could see the whole regiment, all closed up and in order, with the head of the Iowa regiment in sight behind it. While we waited our horses cropped the short grass by the road, and Joss Pettit strolled over to where I was.

"This colonel knows what he's about," he said. Sheridan was still up on the hillock, peering ahead through his field glasses.

"We've covered just as much ground as we would have done if we'd been pressing and hurrying all night. But look at the difference. The whole regiment is closed up. Everybody is fresh. The horses are fresh. Whatever we got to do now, we're in shape to do it."

I tried to figure this out. Apparently the way to make speed was not to be in a hurry about things. Certainly we had had an easy march; yet Joss said we'd gone just as far as we would have done if it had been the usual trot-walk-trot-halt-trot sort of business, and Joss was an old-timer who usually knew what he was talking about.

When Sheridan came down from the hill, things began to happen. One platoon of our company deployed in a mounted skirmish line and trotted on ahead of us, cross-country. The rest of us waited in the road for about five minutes, when a lieutenant came galloping back and said something to Sheridan. Sheridan nodded, and we could see him rapping out orders; then the bugler sounded his calls, the notes sounding unnaturally loud and insistent in the early morning hush.

Now we were in the saddle, and for the first time since

we left camp we were going at a trot. Somewhere on ahead we heard a carbine fired, then another, then half a dozen shots all in one burst. The head of our column came up over the crest of a little hill. In a broad, shallow valley beyond there was a little one-street town, unpainted frame buildings clustering around a railroad station, long rows of boxcars on sidings beyond the station. We could see a few men running about in the street, and in the fields and yards nearer us there were our mounted skirmishers, a few of them firing from the saddle, puffs of smoke from fence corners and houses marking where Rebel skirmishers were firing back.

Then our bugles ordered us to draw sabers, and there was a long metallic rustle down the length of the column; the bugles rang out again, and all of a sudden the whole regiment was going down the road at a furious gallop, and for some reason we were all yelling, with Sheridan out in front of us, swinging his hat. We went pounding through the main street of that little town of Booneville, scattering the handful of Johnnies who were trying to get organized to stop us.

We went clear through the town and drew up, at last, alongside the railroad track, everybody flushed and panting and feeling pleased and excited. My company trotted on for another half mile to picket the roads and fields, in case some more Rebs should come up to recapture the place. Back in town, big columns of black smoke were going up. The Iowa regiment had taken over the railroad station and was setting fire to the freight cars, while patrols were rounding up the Johnnies who were still in town.

I had a squad patrolling a little crossroads, and when I looked back toward town I could see the rest of our regiment getting to work to destroy the railroad.

Sheridan had perhaps four hundred men lined up by the track, the men standing elbow to elbow. At a word of command, the long rank moved forward and each man bent over and grabbed the end of a railroad tie. At another command, everybody straightened up, and a two-hundred-yard section of track was ripped loose, balanced for a moment on the end of its ties, and then tossed over upside down. Then the ties were wrenched loose, built up into big piles, and set on fire. As they burned, the rails were laid across the tops of the piles so that the heat softened the iron and the rails bent out of shape like wet macaroni.

I didn't have a lot of time to watch all of this, because before long we could see dust down the road to the south. I took a couple of men, trotted down to have a look, and quickly found out that the dust was being kicked up by a column of Confederate cavalry. We galloped back to the crossroads, and I rode on to a little farmyard where Captain Alger, our company commander, had established himself. He sent somebody off to tell the colonel, then rode back to the crossroads with me and began to call in our other patrols to form a skirmish line behind a snake-rail fence at the edge of a little field.

The next thing I knew, Sheridan was beside Captain Alger, talking to him and peering down the road. I had begun to get kind of excited, for there seemed to be quite a few Rebs in that approaching column and I didn't see how our one company could begin to handle them, but Sheridan was very matter-of-fact.

"Don't try to stop 'em here, Captain," he was saying. "Just fire enough to make them spread themselves out into line, then fall back to the railroad. We'll wait for 'em there."

After that, things seemed to happen fast. When the head of the Rebel column was maybe a quarter of a mile away we began firing. I don't think we hit anything, but we did make them form a battle line, and we could see the men dismounting and preparing to come forward on foot. We fired some more as they advanced, but before long we turned and rode back, passed the blazing tie piles and the sagging railroad iron, to the far side of the low railway embankment where we dismounted and got ready to fight on foot. One man in every four was detailed to lead four horses to the rear; the rest of us crouched behind the embankment and got our carbines ready.

The Rebs were coming on fast, and there seemed to be a lot of them. Sheridan was riding along our lines, warning the boys to wait until the enemy got in close.

"Plenty of time, boys, plenty of time," he was saying. "Make 'em come to you. Then when you hit 'em, hit 'em with everything you've got."

It seemed to me that we were letting the Johnnies get awfully close, and I was getting more and more nervous. Then somebody yelled: "Now, boys—let 'em have it!" There was a tremendous racket all along the embankment. We were firing our carbines as fast as we could, and the air was full of smoke and quick-spitting spurts of flame, everybody was yelling like mad, and men who had emptied their carbines had pulled out their revolvers and were firing them.

Then the firing died down almost as suddenly as it had begun, and the smoke drifted away. In the field in front of us we could see quite a few Rebs stretched out on the ground, and the rest of them were running away. With our repeating carbines and our revolvers, our one regiment had put more bullets in the air than a whole brigade of infantry could have done. The advancing Confederates had not had a chance in the world.

We jumped on top of the place where the railroad track had been and swung our caps and yelled—then there was a drumming of horses' hoofs, and two of our mounted squadrons went charging out to hurry the retreating Rebs on their way.

The fight was over. Our mounted men chased the Johnnies for half a mile or so, rounding up quite a few prisoners. The colonel organized details to go out and bring in the wounded men and bury the dead. And the first thing anybody knew we were back tearing up more railroad track just as if nothing had happened. That night we were drawn back into the little town while the Iowa regiment moved out to set up picket lines. We had captured Confederate bacon and corn bread for supper, and when we went to sleep we were very well pleased with ourselves.

Next day there was more work on the tracks—in all, I suppose we made a break in that railroad about a mile and a half long—and everything in and around the town of Booneville that could possibly be of any use to the Confederate army was burned or broken in bits or carried away. Then we headed back toward the Federal lines, with a mounted squadron in the rear to watch for pursuing Rebels, and a day later we were back where we had started.

In a way it had been a routine sort of assignment. Every week in the year, somewhere along the front, some cavalry outfit was doing something like this, and there wasn't anything sensational about it. It was just part of the day's work, done competently but not the sort of thing that would win medals for anybody.

Yet it had been a new experience for us. We had covered, in all, about one hundred and fifty miles. We had destroyed Rebel trains and property, we had had a smart little fight, and before we returned we had sent in perhaps two hundred prisoners; and somehow we were in better shape when we got back than we had been when we set out, we had moved fast without hurrying, no horses had foundered from overwork, there had never been any confusion or any mix-ups—all in all, for the first time since we left Benton Barracks we felt that we were really accomplishing something.

We felt proud that we were cavalrymen. When we rode back into the Union lines we swaggered a little, as if we were just as good as anybody else and maybe a lot better than most.

That night, as I got Red's saddle off and got ready to give him a grooming, I suddenly realized something: I'd been through a fight, with Rebs charging and lots of guns going off, and somehow I had been so excited that I'd forgotten to be scared!

9. SWORD OF THE LORD AND OF GIDEON

After that everything seemed to be better.

For one thing, rations picked up. The commissary would bring up fresh onions, potatoes, and beef, as well as salt pork and hardtack, and brought it up more regularly, so we didn't miss a meal once or twice a week the way we used to. We got new clothing, too, and it was high time because what we had been wearing was so dirty and ragged we were ashamed of ourselves. We burned our old stuff, went for a swim in the river, and put on the new. When we lit our pipes after supper and sat around bragging about what we had done in the fight at Booneville, we felt like real soldiers.

About this time the big Sibley tents disappeared and we got pup tents in their place. Each man was given a piece of canvas about six feet by four, with buttons and button-holes along the edges, which he carried with him at all times. At night two men would button their pieces together, run a picket rope between stakes about two feet off the ground, throw the buttoned-together tent halves over it, peg the edges down to the ground—and there was a tent, just big enough for two men to sleep in.

Actually, it wasn't a very good tent. It was open at both ends, you couldn't sit up in it, and if you brushed against the canvas from the inside—which you generally did—the place you had touched would leak. But the big thing was that we always had these tents with us, whereas the Sibleys had to be carried in wagons. When the weather was really bad, so you wanted a tent the most, the wagons were sure to be stuck in the mud ten miles away. If the pup tents were cramped, they were ever so much better than nothing at all. Once we got used to them, we couldn't have been hired to go back to the old system.

Colonel Sheridan made the rounds every day to see that our camp was clean. Rubbish, garbage, and other refuse had to be buried, right off—and for the first time I realized that an army camp didn't really have to stink. Rainstorms no longer sent little rivers running through our tents; the colonel made us dig drainage ditches to carry the water off. We had to put in a lot more time taking care of our horses, and they looked better for it—looked better, and felt better, and therefore stood up better under hard service.

The funny thing was that what worked with the horses seemed to work with the men, too. We were in better spirits, and we didn't get sick as often as we used to. The morning line at the doctor's tent began to shrink. Better food and sanitation probably were mostly responsible, but I can't help thinking that part of it was because we had at last begun to take pride in ourselves and our regiment.

Of course that fight at Booneville wasn't really much of

a fight, and although we did a lot of talking about it we pretty soon found out that it hadn't amounted to much. We found that out because we got into a real fight and then we could see the difference.

This new fight happened at Booneville, just like the other one.

The Rebs had retreated from Corinth, and General Halleck wanted a cavalry outpost down at Booneville to keep an eye on them. So Colonel Sheridan took our regiment and the 2d Iowa down there—officially, our two regiments were a brigade, and Sheridan was in command even though he was only a colonel—and we rode on down and made camp a little north of town and kept patrols out on all the roads leading south.

Right here I personally had another stroke of luck.

Since Sheridan was a brigade commander, he was entitled to have a squad of enlisted men attached to his headquarters to serve as orderlies, messengers, and so on. The day we got to Booneville, Company B was ordered to detail such a squad, and Joss Pettit was told to pick half a dozen men and report at brigade headquarters. I still wasn't a bit sure that tough little man approved of me— but when the detail was posted, I was one of the men he picked.

All the men liked to be on those headquarters details. It meant a good deal of extra work, in some ways, and of course you were right under the colonel's eye, but at the same time you got out of a good many of the ordinary chores, and besides you were where you could hear interesting things and know what was going on.

First thing we found out was that following Sheridan around was apt to keep a man busy.

Right now Sheridan wanted to know everything there was to know about the country near Booneville. He had to know where every road and lane went, where the creeks ran and how much deeper they got after a heavy rain. He found out where there were swamps, where the woodlots and cornfields and back pastures were. He had to know where all the farmhouses were and the names of the people who lived in them. He would make somebody follow every twisting cowpath or footpath there was so that he could know exactly what lay at the other end of it; he knew where the ground was low and where there were hills and ridges; and he made lots of sketch maps.

What's more, he insisted that we orderlies and messengers had to know as much about these things as he himself.

"When we have a fight, you boys have got to move fast," he told us. "You won't have time to ask your way. You've got to *know*. I'll lift the scalp of the first man who gets lost." He glanced at the stripes on my sleeve, and added grimly: "Or his chevrons, if he has any."

Then he began to talk to us enlisted men just as if we were officers.

"The Rebs have a dozen chances to surprise us," he said. "They know this country as if it was their own back yard. One of these days they're going to try to run us out of here. We've got to know every single way by which they can come at us. We've got to know this territory just as well as if we'd been raised here. If I tell one of you boys to take a note to Major Whittaker or Captain Samuels, you've got to know right where they are and you've got to know the quickest way to reach 'em. The safety of the whole brigade may depend on how well you do your jobs."

So we did a lot of riding. There were patrols on every road, and picket posts in a chain clear around the town. At all hours Sheridan would go to see that they were on the job. Some of us always had to ride with him.

I liked it. Not being in the middle of a big solid column, this was almost like riding for pleasure. I got the notion that Red felt the same way about it—as if he and I were getting away from camp routine for a while and taking a canter out on an empty road, without others ahead of us to kick up a dust. Life almost began to be fun.

One hot morning we were on the edge of a big swamp, south of town, and Sheridan pointed to a low wooded ridge, half a mile on the other side of the swamp.

"Corporal," he said, looking at me and pointing at the ridge, "take a couple of men and find the quickest way to get across that swamp."

I picked Lance Huntington and Red Miller, and we set out.

I was excited, at first—getting an order direct from Sheridan somehow made you feel all set up and important —but this was a miserable assignment. The swamp looked nightmarish, with spiky dead trees coming up out of scummy water, and tangled vines and briars wherever there was dry ground. Snakes slid off dead logs as we approached. The air was hot and heavy and full of gnats and mosquitoes.

We couldn't force our horses through anywhere, so after a while we tied them on dry ground and tried to get through on foot. It didn't seem to me that any man in his senses would ever want to cross that swamp, but the colonel had said to find the quickest way so I had to keep looking for it even if I didn't think there was a quickest way, or a longest way either.

We got wet and muddy, ripped our uniforms on thorns and jagged branches, and Lance got stuck to his thighs in squelchy mud. It took us five minutes to pull him out. When we did, one of his boots stayed in the mud and it took another five minutes to find it.

About midafternoon we were ready to quit. I hated to go back and tell the colonel that there just wasn't any way across that blasted swamp, but there didn't seem to be any help for it. We were sitting on a log on a kind of bushy island at the edge of the swamp, catching our breath, when at last I told the others to stay there a few minutes— I wanted to take one final look before admitting that I hadn't been able to do what Sheridan had told me to do.

I went prowling off through the brush, not heading anywhere in particular. I got into a tangle of tall, weedy stuff that was like nothing I ever saw in Michigan, pushed my way through—and there, right in front of me, was the most ramshackle little cabin I ever saw in my life, with dead ashes on a stone fireplace in front of it, and a little makeshift bench by the trunk of a scrub pine. There were fish scales on the ground, all over, and there was a smell of fish in the air—although the whole swamp smelled so bad it was hard to notice.

I stared at this for a couple of minutes before I realized what it was. There'd been lots of campfire talk about how every marsh and jungle in Mississippi had hidden cabins where Negroes lived—runaway slaves, mostly, although they said some of them were free Negroes. These people hid out and never let white folks see them, but they did trust Union soldiers. I'd heard lots of stories about how some of our boys who had been wounded or lost and were trying to get back to our lines were helped by these people. The boys swore that any colored man you met, except maybe some of the house servants in the big plantation mansions, would help a Union soldier if he could. So I looked around a little, and then I called out:

"Anybody here? I'm a Union soldier."

It seemed ridiculous, calling out in that dead swamp. But I had hardly finished before a skinny colored man wearing nothing but a ragged pair of breeches slid out of the undergrowth ten yards away. I suppose he had been watching me all the time.

We looked at each other, and finally he said:

"You lost, Captain? You hurt?"

"I'm not hurt and I'm not lost," I said. "I just want to find a way across this swamp."

He wrinkled his forehead and seemed puzzled, and pointed back over my shoulder.

"Town's that way," he said. "Lots of Lincoln soldiers there."

I told him I knew that, and explained how the colonel had sent me to find the quickest way across to the ridge. The colored man looked suspicious.

"What for he wants that?" he demanded.

Well, I told him, we were going to fight the Rebs pretty soon, and the colonel had to know all the short cuts; maybe the Rebs would whip us if he didn't. The man seemed doubtful so I went over it two or three times, laying it on heavy. At last I guess it made sense to him. He said there was a way across the swamp and he would show it to me. And he said his name was Mose.

He led me back away from the cabin, passing the log where the other two troopers were, so I told them to come along. We tramped on after Mose, clear back to the dry ground on the town side of the swamp, coming out near where our horses were. I asked Mose if horses could use the path. He said they could, so we untied our horses and mounted.

It didn't seem right for all of us to be riding while our guide walked, so I told Mose to get up behind me. He looked surprised, then shook his head emphatically; he mumbled something about how the Lincoln soldiers should ride and he'd walk on ahead. I couldn't change him, so that was the way we went.

The way Mose took zigzagged and wandered all over. We never could have found it by ourselves if we'd hunted all year. It was a good way, though, that finally came out on dry rising ground on the far side of the swamp. We kept on until we hit the ridge itself, and scrambled up to the crest where we found a little country road.

It seemed to me we'd been on this road a day or so earlier, and I thought it went north for a couple of miles, then struck a turnpike that ran to Booneville. I figured Colonel Sheridan would want to know what we found when we got to the ridge, so I told Lance to ride north until he hit the turnpike, then get back to camp that way. Lance was pretty doubtful, but I told him to get moving and not to argue with corporals, so pretty soon he set out.

Then Red and I followed Mose back across the swamp.

As we rode back I began to worry. We'd found the shortest way across the swamp all right—in fact, Mose said it was the only way—but I knew perfectly well we never could find it again in all the world unless Mose was along to show it to us. When we got back to our starting place I told Mose to come on into camp with us, because Colonel Sheridan would need him as a guide. I went on to say that we could find an extra pair of pants, a shirt or two for him, and maybe even a pair of shoes, to say nothing of a sack of hardtack and a side of bacon.

I didn't need to argue so hard. Mose was perfectly willing to come. I didn't know whether it was because he wanted the things we could give him or whether he just figured the Lincoln soldiers were his friends. Whatever it was, he came back to camp with us.

It was late in the day when we got there, and we must have looked queer—two muddy soldiers riding in with a half-naked colored man in tow. The headquarters crowd gave us a good laugh. When Sheridan stepped out of his tent he chuckled, too, and called us over.

When I told him how we had crossed the swamp he looked surprised, and said he hadn't figured we could do it; he had thought the swamp was impassable and had sent us on our trip to prove it. He asked Mose all sorts of questions, and told us to hang onto him and fix him up with a place to stay. Then he called to the brigade quartermaster to make sure there was a mule for Mose to ride.

"You never know," he said. "One of these days it might be real important to have that colored boy guiding a mounted column for us."

As it turned out it was important, and right soon, too.

We hardly got the day started next morning before a courier came pelting in from a picket post south of town with the news that a big column of Rebel cavalry was coming up.

Sheridan began scribbling messages and we couriers galloped off with them. Sheridan had two squadrons of the Iowa regiment ride south to peck away at that Rebel column and find out how big it was. He told the Michigan regiment to form south of town and await orders. Patrol detachments were called in, the brigade wagon trains were pulled up close to headquarters, and Lance Huntington was started on a fifteen-mile ride to the nearest Federal infantry camp with a note of warning.

When the Iowa boys reported, things looked bad. The Rebs had a whole cavalry division, four or five thousand men, with artillery, and they were coming on as if they meant business. Sheridan didn't have nine hundred men in his whole brigade.

But somehow he didn't seem worried.

"We can handle 'em if we can keep 'em off our flanks," he said, thoughtfully. "I don't care how many they've got, we can lick 'em if we can make 'em keep in front of us."

After a lot more galloping with messages, Sheridan had a battle line strung out down below town across the road the Rebs were using. The right end of this line rested on the edge of my pet swamp, and the other end was in another swamp, a quarter of a mile to the east—so they said, anyhow: I never saw it. The troopers were all dismounted, with the horses tethered off to the rear, except for a couple of squadrons under Captain Alger which Sheridan held back as a sort of reserve.

Sheridan was all over the place, making sure that everybody was where he was supposed to be. When he had finished a final ride along the line, he jerked his head at me.

"Corporal, get hold of that colored guide of yours," he said. "Put him on his mule and keep him right with you. Then both of you wait right here until I call for you."

"Right here" was a knoll a little behind the firing line, where field headquarters had been established. There was nothing much there except some orderlies and a few spare horses, an ambulance carrying some headquarters equipment, an officer or two and an enlisted clerk, and a United States flag with its staff stuck in the ground. I dug up Mose, got his mule, and we perched on this knoll to see what would happen next.

The Rebs came up on foot, just like infantry, reminding me of what Joss Pettit had said about dragoon fighting, 'way back at recruit camp. Here were two cavalry commands getting into a big fight, with all the horses off at the rear.

From the knoll I couldn't see much but I could hear a lot—a tremendous racket of musketry and a great many soldiers yelling as loud as they could. Cavalry carbines are awfully good weapons but they have very short barrels and are no good except at close range, so Sheridan made our men wait until the Johnnies were almost on top of them before they fired. When they did fire, though, the Rebels' attack broke all to pieces. With their carbines and revolvers together, every man in our line could get off ten or a dozen shots in one minute, and no attacking line could stand that.

So it was just the way Sheridan had said: as long as we could keep the Rebs in front of us we could beat them, because, even if they did have five men to our one, we could fire ten bullets to their one. We were badly outnumbered, but in a straight toe-to-toe fight we were actually stronger than they were.

The trouble was that the Rebs weren't obliging enough to keep on fighting our kind of fight. As soon as they saw they couldn't break our line they began shifting to the east to get around our left flank. Sheridan's patrols brought him warning.

Sheridan was standing talking to Captain Alger not half a dozen yards from where Mose and I were waiting, and I could hear what he was saying.

"Another hour and they'll be in our rear, and if they get there we're whipped," Sheridan said. "We've got to hit their rear first. That'll pull their flanking column back."

He pointed west, toward my swamp.

"I'll give you a guide who'll show you a path through that swamp," he said. "You'll come out on a road that runs along that ridge there. Turn left on that road and in five minutes you'll be right square in the Rebels' rear. When you get there, have everybody holler like hell and ride straight through 'em. I don't care much whether you kill any Rebels or not. I just want you to make a great big racket. Understand?"

Captain Alger nodded, and Sheridan beckoned to me. I was to take Mose, and we were to lead Captain Alger's squadrons through the swamp. The last thing we heard from Sheridan was: "And *quick*, do you hear? Quick!"

I was all excited and I think Captain Alger was, too, but Mose was cool as a cucumber. He was riding bareback, with no harness except a halter and a shortened picket rope, but he and that mule seemed to have worked out some sort of understanding. They went jogging on ahead as if we were setting out on a Sunday-school picnic. Sheridan had told me to keep my revolver drawn and if Mose led us wrong I was to shoot him, but I never thought that was going to happen and it didn't. Mose took us through that tangle as easily as I would have led someone from my uncle's store down to the steamboat dock, and in a few minutes we were riding up through the trees on the ridge south of the swamp.

Mose and I rode out into the empty road, with Captain Alger on our heels, and looked off to the left. We could hear the racket of the battle, beyond the treetops—the two lines were firing at long range, and the noise wasn't awfully loud—but we couldn't see a thing. The captain brought his command out into the road and formed it in column of fours. In five minutes he was all ready.

Sheridan had sent a dozen extra buglers along to help make the big noise he wanted, and Alger had them spaced along the column. When a cavalry brigade is in action, the brigade bugler will sound a call and each regiment's bugler will repeat it, after which the squadron buglers will sound it. Although he didn't have a hundred and fifty troopers, Alger had enough buglers to sound like a couple of brigades.

We waited there in the sandy road, with the mounted

column bunched up behind us, and the noise of the firing coming flat and sort of unreal over the trees. Then the captain signaled to his bugler. The sharp, quick call rang out down the road, the other buglers picked it up, and the notes went echoing back and forth. Although I had heard those calls dozens of times, I could feel the hair on the back of my neck stirring. I thought: Now it's coming—now we're going to charge—now we're going to have to ride straight into the Rebel lines, with everybody shooting, and, oh Lord, help me not to run away. . . .

Then we were going down the road at a gallop, everybody yelling, hoofbeats drumming in the dirt, bugles blaring like kingdom-coming. We swung out into an open field, and there we were, right behind the Rebs' main battle line. We were riding hard, yelling and sounding the bugles, and I remembered Sunday-school lessons back home about the men who charged the Philistines' camp shouting: "The sword of the Lord and of Gideon!"

Away off to our left Sheridan heard us, and had everybody in his line fire as fast as he could, whether he had anything to shoot at or not, so that the noise of battle suddenly rose as if a lot of new troops had come into action. Captain Alger was swinging his saber and shouting; I was riding right behind him; for some crazy reason Mose was rocketing along on his mule beside me. He had no business being in the front of a charging column but there he was, his eyes flashing and his face shining with sweat, yelling as hard as any of us, beating the flank of his mule with a crumpled slouch hat somebody had given him.

Then we cut off to the left, but I don't quite know what happened next because everything was dust and smoke and noise and quick movement. The first thing I knew we were back with our own men, the Rebs were going off in retreat, and Sheridan had the Iowa regiment mounted to help the Rebs on their way. We had won the battle, and everybody was cheering and laughing. When Sheridan rode past we swung our caps and yelled until our throats hurt.

Sheridan shook his fist and yelled: "Boys, I knew you could do it! I knew you could whip 'em!"

I felt especially good, because if I hadn't stumbled onto Mose by his little cabin the day before, Captain Alger's column could never have got into the Rebels' rear, and the sword of the Lord and of Gideon wouldn't have worked so well.

10.   TO CARRY THE FLAG

The fight at Booneville was some sort of milestone for me.

When the bugles sounded in that road on the ridge and we wheeled out to ride for the Rebel camp, I was just as scared as I had always imagined I would be—but somehow I had gone in with the rest, and nobody but me knew how scared I was. I hadn't turned tail and run, the way I'd been afraid I'd do. I had done what I was supposed to do.

To be sure, I hadn't really done any fighting at all. All I'd done was ride and yell. I don't think a single Rebel fired at me, and the charge we made surprised the enemy so much that hardly any of Captain Alger's men were hurt. But I didn't know it was going to be that way when the charge started. I was frightened then, and yet I'd managed to tuck my fright down out of sight where it didn't show, and secretly I was a little proud that I'd been able to do it. Also, I was the one who had found the way across the swamp; or at least I'd found Mose, who knew the way; so, all in all, I figured Booneville was a big day for me.

Our brigade stayed there for a while after the fight, and they sent another regiment of cavalry, some artillery, and an infantry regiment to strengthen us. But the Rebs didn't bother us again, and before long we moved over to the neighborhood of a town called Rienzi.

Here we got a lot more drill and a great deal of scouting and patrolling. Once our regiment was ordered out on a raid where we captured a big herd of the Rebs' beef cattle, along with a couple of hundred mules. Yet nothing out of the ordinary happened to us, and about the only thing that I remember very clearly is that Sheridan got a new horse.

One of our officers had brought this horse with him from Michigan. The animal was a big gelding, jet-black except for three white ankles, hardly broken to the saddle. When he stood at the picket rope, he had a way of rolling his eyes and tilting his ears and mincing around stiff-legged that made people think he had a mean disposition. The man who owned him, I think, was really a little scared of him. Anyway, he never used him, and one day this summer he led him over to brigade headquarters and gave him to Sheridan.

Sheridan took to the horse at once. Although he was never a graceful horseman, he could ride anything you could saddle and he soon showed that this animal's bad disposition was largely imaginary. All the horse needed was a little work, which under Sheridan he got all right, the same as everybody else did.

Sheridan named him Rienzi, after the town where we were then, and all the rest of the war Rienzi was his favorite mount. Rienzi seemed to be tireless, so strong that even at an ordinary walk he would cover five miles in an hour, and before Sheridan got through with him he was the most famous animal in the Union army. I think, since then, that only Robert E. Lee's famous Traveler and Stonewall Jackson's Little Sorrel were better known than Rienzi.

It was a little while after this that something important happened to me personally. It was about six weeks after the fight at Booneville, but it grew out of that battle so it's what I think of first when I think of the battle.

Sheridan was a brigadier general now and a little swallowtail flag with a star in it flew over his headquarters tent, so when anybody wanted to find him they just looked for that flag. But since Sheridan never stayed at headquarters if any action was going on, it occurred to him that the flag ought to follow him all the time instead of being fastened over an empty tent.

That was where I came in.

I had just finished grooming Red one morning, and had explained to that choosy horse that if he couldn't eat his piece of hardtack without sugar he'd have to go without, because I didn't have any more sugar. I was sitting on a bale of hay working some neat's-foot oil into my saddle when Sergeant Pettit stuck his head around the corner of the stables.

"General wants you," he said, jerking his thumb.

I went off in a hurry—it never was a good idea to keep Sheridan waiting. As I came up in front of his tent he came out of it.

"Whatever happened to that colored man who took you through the swamp?" he asked, unexpectedly.

I explained that Mose had gone back to his cabin, equipped with new pants, half a wagon of rations, a good rifle, and a chest of ammunition. He could have come with us, but he wanted to stay where he was.

"All right," said Sheridan. Then he dismissed that subject.

"Starting today," he said, "you're my orderly. You're not on the brigade headquarters staff; you're on mine. I don't want you to do the things orderlies usually do. I got other men to put up my tent and take care of my horses and so on. What I want you to do is carry my flag."

He glanced up at the starred swallowtail on its staff in front of the tent.

"Wherever I ride, I want you to be right behind me with that flag," he said. "There'll be special jobs, too, now and then, but the main thing is to carry the flag. No matter *where* I go, that flag has to be right with me. Always. Understand?"

"Yes, sir."

"Good." All of a sudden he grinned and slapped me on the shoulder.

"Nice job you did, Corporal!" he said. "I don't forget things like that. You ride with me and you'll do some riding. You'll have some fun, too!"

He turned to go back into the tent.

"Sergeant Pettit will fix the papers," he said.

I wandered down to the stables, half in a daze. No soldier could ask for better luck. Nine-tenths of the drudgery that goes with army life would miss me from now on. Any general's official family led an envied life, even the privates who did the headquarters chores, and this job I was getting was better than being an officer in lots of ways. Who wouldn't give his eyeteeth to ride at Phil Sheridan's heels, carrying his flag?

I said all of this to Joss Pettit, and he chuckled.

"You made out your will, have you?" he asked.

"Why?"

"You didn't see much of Sheridan in the Booneville fight, did you? No, you were off most of the time with Captain Alger's column. Well, if there was a hot place anywhere along the firing line that Colonel Sheridan didn't get into, it was only because he hadn't heard about it. You ride behind him and you'll see more action than all the rest of the regiment put together. It'll be a lot of fun—while it lasts."

I hadn't thought of this, and my face probably showed it. Joss went on relentlessly.

"Why do you suppose he wants a special orderly just to carry his flag? Most generals stay close to headquarters when a fight's on. If they have to go anywheres, they just detail whoever's handy to carry the flag. But Sheridan has to have a full-time man for it. Why? Because he's *always* going to be out on the firing line, that's why."

Joss thought of something else.

"That big Rienzi can go so fast, all the bullets they fire at Sheridan will miss him. You know who they'll hit? They'll hit the fellow that comes at his heels, carrying his flag."

Joss went on and on like that, until I had to admit that carrying Sheridan's flag didn't look like the healthiest job in the whole army. But, then and there, I vowed that I'd let a dozen bullets hit me before I showed the white feather. No matter where he had me go, General Sheridan was not going to know that I was afraid—not even if I was scared to death!

That was the day orders came through for General Sheridan to take the 2d Michigan Cavalry and four infantry regiments and go to Kentucky just as quickly as he could.

A Confederate army led by General Braxton Bragg had made a big circle around to the east and had got nearly up to the Ohio River. If it ever really got there, the North might lose the war. General Buell had managed to get a Union army up to Louisville to head Bragg off, but he was afraid he didn't have enough men to fight him so he asked General Grant, who commanded all of us down in Mississippi, to send help. That was why Sheridan was to hurry north with these five regiments.

The only thing worse than marching some place, in the army, was going there by train.

We usually got dirty old freight cars to ride in, and we had a lot of trouble loading our horses and fixing them up so that they'd still be alive when we finished our trip. Then there was always our horse furniture to load, the smiths' outfits, forage and rations, and so on, and always a big hurry about it even though, when we finally got loaded, we would sit on the sidetracks for several hours before anything happened.

It was the same this time as any other, except that being one of the general's orderlies made things different for me personally.

One freight car was set aside for the general's own horses, another carried nothing but headquarters baggage, and there were plenty of us to do the work, so everything went smoothly. After we got everything loaded, and our own stuff put away in a spare corner of the headquarters car, we sat on the car roof swinging our heels and watching everybody else work.

Down the platform we could see two officers walking along, arguing. One of them was Sheridan. Short as the general was, the officer with him didn't seem to be any taller. The two were talking had about something, and, when we could see their faces, they looked angry.

The man beside me nudged me in the ribs with his elbow.

"Know who that is with the general?" he asked. "That's U. S. Grant!"

I'd never seen him before and I took a good look. He had a sandy little beard, and was stoop-shouldered. He was wearing a private's blouse with a rusty pair of shoulder straps and he had a stub of a cigar in his teeth. All in all, he looked like a farmer. As the two men came nearer we could hear him saying:

"There'll be lots of active campaigning here soon. I'd like to have you stay here."

Sheridan's face was always dark, but when he was angry it got almost mahogany-colored, and that was the way it was now.

"I'll be more useful in Kentucky—sir," he rasped. The "sir" came out like an afterthought. "That's where the fighting's going to be. Besides, that's how my orders read."

They walked on where we couldn't hear any more, Sheridan gesturing with his hands. We found out later that we had heard part of what was probably the only personal disagreement those two generals ever had. Grant wanted to keep Sheridan in his army; Sheridan figured nothing was going to happen in Mississippi and wanted to fight, so naturally he insisted on going to Kentucky. Grant couldn't make him stay, but he was trying to talk him into it and wasn't getting anywhere.

We got started, at last. The trip was as hot and uncomfortable as such things always were . . . only at the stops, when we took the horses out to feed and water them, I found out once more that a lot of those army chores go a good deal easier if you're working direct for the commanding general. People don't get in your way so much.

We got to Louisville eventually, and it was a madhouse —streets full of soldiers, hotel lobbies and bars full of generals, with nobody seeming to know where to go or what to do. The place was so full of rumors that if you stood around long enough you could hear anything, including a report that one hundred thousand Rebels had crossed the Ohio River and were marching to capture Cleveland. We heard one crazy story about two Union major generals who had a quarrel in a hotel lobby. One had pulled a revolver and killed the other, and nothing could be done to him because he was a pal of the governor of Indiana. (That crazy story, by the way, turned out to be true.)

Troops were being reshuffled all over the place and nobody seemed to know who commanded what. The regiments Sheridan had brought with him were reassigned, and the 2d Michigan was sent off into some cavalry brigade, but that didn't affect Joss and me because we were on permanent detail to General Sheridan. Then one day we found out that Sheridan had been given command of an infantry division—three whole brigades, a dozen regiments in all, plus some artillery. Right after that the army pulled itself out of Louisville and went hurrying down to the southeast looking for General Bragg. When we found him, I learned why Joss had said that I ought to make my will.

11. THE END OF A QUARREL

The weather was hot. Most of the ponds and streams were dry, and it was hard to get water. We moved in a big, choking cloud of dust that got in our hair, our eyes and noses, and seeped in under our clothing. We felt gritty inside and out, and it was easy to get mad about things. Buell had close to sixty thousand soldiers, they said, and at night the whole sky would glow with the light of their campfires, so you couldn't see the stars.

The Confederates, off to the east somewhere, were trying to get out of Kentucky while we were trying to head them off. But nobody knew quite where they were, so we were groping blindly to find them, covering all the roads and spilling out all over the countryside.

Sheridan was busier than ever. When he wasn't trotting up and down the marching column himself, he was sending messages all over, so that on days when the division marched fifteen miles some of his couriers and aides would travel fifty.

At night, after we'd made camp, Sheridan was still on the move, seeing that everything was just so and talking to the men who commanded his brigades. I always had to ride with him, carrying his flag, which seemed kind of silly to me until I caught on to what he was trying to do. None of the soldiers in his division had ever seen him or heard of him before, and he wanted them all to know what he looked like; when he rode through the camps he'd have his flag with him so that they could identify him as the division commander. He used to say that no officer could expect his men to follow him if they didn't know him by sight. He was going to have to take this division into battle soon, and when that happened he wanted everybody to look for the general and his flag; because when the fight came he wasn't going to *send* his men in—he was going to *lead* them in.

You were always learning something new and unexpected about Sheridan.

I remember one evening he'd ridden back to the wagon train, three or four miles in the rear. His constant checking up on his wagons was one reason his outfits didn't run short of rations or ammunition the way others did. He had taken a couple of staff officers and several couriers, but he had sent everybody off on errands and when he started back I was the only one with him. Since he was a general and I was a corporal, of course I rode a few paces behind him.

We were crossing the camp of some other division, and we passed a campfire where several officers were standing around, talking. All of a sudden Sheridan looked hard at one of these officers—a brigadier general, he was, young-ish, good-looking, with a trim little beard and mustache, tall and slim. Sheridan reined in his horse, jumped off, handed the reins to me, and ran over to him.

The general looked up and stared at Sheridan for a minute; then he recognized him, and from the look on his face you could see he was in doubt whether Sheridan was going to hit him or hug him. Sheridan came up, stood looking at him for a minute, and then stuck out his hand. The other general took it, they both began to laugh, and they shook hands like long-lost friends. The other officers were introduced, and they began to talk together. Finally Sheridan shook the brigadier general's hand once more, clapped him on the shoulder, came back and mounted Rienzi, and we rode off.

This time Sheridan didn't keep in front of me. He rode beside me, just as if I was another officer, and pretty soon he began to talk. (Sheridan could be like that, not paying any attention to rank: I've known him to go up to a trooper and borrow a plug of tobacco, or stop by a campfire for a cup of coffee with the privates just as natural as if he'd never worn shoulder straps.)

"That's Bill Terrill," Sheridan said. "He was at West Point when I was. I came within an inch of murdering him once. I could have been thrown out of the army on account of him; I could have gone to prison for what I did. I used to hate him worse'n anybody alive."

He chuckled. "I learned something, too," he said. "I learned how to keep my temper."

I wanted to ask him more about it, but I didn't know if I should. In a minute he went on to tell me.

"He was cadet sergeant in my company at the academy. Used to ride me all the time. He was from Virginia, and had that damned aristocratic manner all those Virginia cadets had, so I hated him.

"Anyhow, one day on the parade ground he was on me, hard. Nothing I did was right. We were standing in ranks, with fixed bayonets, and he claimed I wasn't doing the manual right and called me a half-witted Mick from the canal. I got so mad I jumped out of ranks and lunged at him with my bayonet."

He was silent for a moment, then I heard him chuckle again in the dark.

"I really was going to kill him," Sheridan said. "I was too mad to think. I was going to kill him.

"But as I started to swing, something stopped me. I came to my senses just one second before it would have been too late. I slammed the butt of my musket down and stood there, glaring at him, quivering all over, partly because I was mad and partly because I was frightened at how close I'd come to committing murder.

"Well, after the company was dismissed, Terrill called me over to a spot behind the barracks and we went at it with our fists."

Again I heard that little chuckle.

"He beat the daylights out of me," he said. "His arms were too long for me. I couldn't get at him——"

"You should've got in close and grappled with him," I broke in, remembering Joss Pettit's advice. "Then you could have brought up your knee, or——" I suddenly remembered that he was a general and I was a corporal, and I stopped, all confused. I could feel myself getting red all the way down to my waist. I wanted to jump off my horse and run and hide some place. Sheridan reined in and stared at me. Then he threw his head back and laughed.

"You're dead right," he said, finally. "Trouble was, I was too angry to think. . . . Anyhow, somebody reported us. I was brought up before the superintendent on charges and it could have been bad—I could have gone to prison. As it was, I got off easy; they suspended me from the Academy for one year, but I did go back and graduate a year behind my class."

There was a little silence, then Sheridan continued:

"I've never really lost my temper since. Lots of times I've lost a little of it, lots more times I've pretended to lose it, but that was the last time I got so angry I didn't know what I was doing.

"I hadn't seen Bill Terrill from the day I was suspended until just now. I'd heard that when Virginia seceded he didn't go with his state; stuck with the army, instead, and now he's a general. And so am I. We got a big fight ahead of us, tomorrow or next day, so when I saw him there I thought I'd just go over and shake hands."

I don't know that anything ever set me up much more than having Phil Sheridan confide in me like that. I couldn't have felt prouder if I'd been six feet tall. As we rode back to headquarters, I thought: Sheridan had had something to lick, too; he had had to lick his temper like I've got to lick my fear. He did it, so I can do it, too.

We'd camped that night near a little stream called Doctor's Creek, which still had some pools of water, and beyond our lines the creek ran into the Chaplin River near the town of Perryville. Before we got to bed a courier came up with orders from headquarters: at dawn Sheridan was to push across the creek and on to the river.

It was just getting light when the drums beat the long roll next morning. It always made a little shiver go down my spine, when the drums went like that. Headquarters drummers began it, the drummers at brigade and regimental headquarters took it up, and they all went on and on and on, insistent, maddening, never stopping. Men stumbled up from their blankets, buttoning coats, reaching for their muskets, and officers buckled on their swords, ran for the company lines, noncoms gesturing and bawling out orders, orderlies hurrying up from the picket ropes with horses for the field officers and generals.

In a few minutes the brigade lines were formed, and the leading regiment fanned out into a wide skirmish line, going on out of sight in the broken country to the east. After a bit the whole brigade started after it, regiments bunched up in solid masses, ready to run out and form battle lines in any direction. We began to hear skirmish fire—a shot here and another there, two or three cracking out together, a few scattered singles, then several more in a cluster, as the skirmishers crept forward through the woods and the clearings, spaced three or four yards apart, feeling to see where the enemy was and how many of him there were.

Pretty soon Sheridan swung into the saddle, calling to a couple of officers to go with him. I'd been watching him, so as soon as he was mounted I mounted, too, hanging onto that battle flag, falling in behind him when he started to move.

He headed straight toward the firing, which was growing heavier, and we hadn't ridden a hundred yards before he sent a courier with orders for a battery of artillery to follow us. Then we went splashing through the creek, following a sandy road that led up a gentle slope toward a chain of low hills a mile away.

Now we caught up with the skirmishers. The Rebs had fallen back, but at the base of the hills they were giving us a steady long-range fire—noisy, but not doing much damage just yet. Sheridan scribbled orders on a little tablet and sent people galloping off with them. As the guns he'd sent for came pounding up, he rode over to the battery commander and gestured with his hat in his hand to show where he wanted them.

There was a big hullaballoo, a lot of shouting and racket while the guns went into position—there never was anything more exciting than to see a six-gun battery go into action in a hurry—and in a minute or two they were banging away at the Johnnies on the hills.

When the first of Sheridan's brigades came up, he shook it out into a long line that went rolling up the slope, Sheridan right in the middle of it (and me right at his heels). Sheridan had been told to hold the ground beyond the creek, so he figured the only way to do it was to take those hills.

He got them without much trouble, because there weren't many Rebs in the way, but the whole Rebel army was just a little beyond the hills and Sheridan no sooner had his division posted on the high ground than the Rebs decided to chase him off. Suddenly we were in the middle of the hottest fight I'd ever dreamed of.

I thought we had had some smart fighting there at

Booneville, but that was a quiet church social compared to what we got now, and I began to see why the infantry always claimed that the cavalry had things easy.

The Rebs were firing a lot of artillery. There was a spiteful, hateful sound in the noise exploding shell made —it made me want to cut and run more than any other single thing on the battlefield. Before long the infantry firing lines came in close, the rifle fire grew so loud and continuous you couldn't hear the shell, and the whole field got hot and foggy with powder smoke so that half the time you couldn't see fifty feet.

We seemed to be far out in front of the rest of the army. Several times couriers brought messages from corps headquarters warning Sheridan not to bring on a general engagement. Each time he read one of these, Sheridan would swear terribly, then he'd have an aide write a polite reply saying he couldn't bring on an engagement because the Confederates were doing it instead.

Sheridan was out along the firing lines most of the time. Wherever things seemed to be the worst, with the Rebs firing fastest and getting in closest, Sheridan was sure to go galloping up with his hat crumpled in his fist, his dark face glistening with sweat, encouraging the men, holding them to their work, letting them see for themselves that their commanding officer was right up there taking everything they had to take.

Sometimes he'd bring artillery up to some threatened spot, staying there himself to show just where the guns should be placed. Sometimes he'd steady a nervous infantry colonel, or show him where to put his men so that their fire would be more effective. When he saw men drifting back to the rear, white-faced and scared, he'd either raise their spirits with a joke or a friendly word, so that they'd turn around and get back into the fight of their own accord, or he'd blast them with hot fury and swing his sword as if he meant to cut them down, so that they simply didn't dare run away again.

I think that was the big thing, being with Sheridan: you didn't dare show the white feather. Riding at his heels that day, always up by the firing line, scared me worse than anything that has ever happened to me before or since. Being on horseback made it twice as bad because most of the soldiers on both sides usually fired a little high. Bullets which would miss a crouching line of infantry could easily wing a mounted man.

How the bullets missed us that day I still don't know. The air seemed to be full of them, and they made an ugly whining sound that kept reminding you how bad they could hurt if they hit you. The only thing that kept me from riding for the rear as fast as I could go was the fact that I just didn't dare. I was afraid of that battle—but I was more afraid of looking like a coward in front of Phil Sheridan. So I stayed with him all day, but that day seemed a year long.

I don't really know who won that fight. We were still on our hills when night came, and the next day the Johnnies had all gone away, but the fight never seemed to be one our army was very proud of. Not long afterward General Buell was removed from command, which I suppose meant that the government wasn't satisfied.

I think what I remember best was riding up the hill that evening to the place where the headquarters tents were being pitched, after the firing had stopped. The general's party—himself, aides, and couriers—was clumping along, everybody pretty winded, when all at once Sheridan turned and looked at me.

"Still got that flag, Corporal?"

I had held onto that dratted flagstaff so hard and so long my hand and wrist were all numb. I waggled the thing a little and said: "Yessir."

"How'd you get along?" he asked. I wanted to make out that I was a big brave soldier, but I was just too tired to pretend any longer, and I said what I didn't intend to say.

"General, I was scared all the time."

Sheridan grinned, and just then it seemed as if I knew him as well as I'd ever known anybody in all my life.

"I get scared, too," he said suddenly. "Everybody does. You can't help that. The big thing is just to go ahead and do what you've got to do anyway."

And that was another milestone for me.

So Sheridan got scared, too! I wasn't the only one, then, who had to pretend to be brave. I began to see, dimly, that what you do is set up your ideal of the man you wish you were, and act as if you really were that sort of man—and maybe, in the end, it comes true for you.

That evening an officer from another division rode over to tell Sheridan that Bill Terrill had been killed in the day's fighting. He and Sheridan had ended their long quarrel on the last day of his life.

12. *THE GIRL IN THE VALLEY*

The Shenandoah Valley runs off southwest from where the Blue Ridge meets the Potomac River. It's the prettiest country I ever saw, miles and miles of it, with long blue mountains on each side, and cool, almost as cool as back home in Michigan. In the evening the dusk lies thick while the mountains are still bright with the last of the sunlight, and you can sit and watch and feel that something wonderful will happen if you just wait for it.

Down the middle of the Valley, running from the Potomac all the way to Staunton, goes a main road they call the Valley Pike. Before the army wagons and artillery cut it up, it was a good road, with an oiled surface of packed gravel, better for marching than most of the roads we had traveled.

The road goes through good farming country, with nice houses and big barns, rolling green pastures and golden-brown fields of grain. By the time we got there, most of the fences had been destroyed so the country was all open like a big park.

The towns along the Valley Pike aren't like the places I

was used to. Winchester, Strasburg, Harrisonburg, and the other places—they looked neat and trim, as if they'd come out of a picture book. There were white frame houses with green shutters, built right up against the street with shaded lawns behind them; and big brick houses that looked as if they had been there a long time and had been lived in by people who went to lots of pains to take good care of them.

Everything looked finished. There weren't any fields of ragged stumps or spindly second-growth timber, like we had around all the little towns in Michigan, or mean-looking little villages straggling discouraged-like along a dirt road like the ones we'd seen in Mississippi.

You never really know where you are going, when you start off to war. The road that leads you up to the recruiting office keeps on going, taking you to places you never thought about when you started out. It seemed to me afterward that it was this Valley Pike that I'd been marching toward ever since I left home. I'd been heading for it when we were moving down through Missouri, when we were scouting south across Tennessee, when we fought the Rebs and burned railroad trains and gumshoed through the swamps in Mississippi. All the fighting that came after Perryville—terrible fighting, worse than anything I'd ever dreamed of, so bad that it changed something 'way down inside of us and turned us from gawky boys into grown men full of a miserable kind of knowledge we'd have been glad to forget—all of that, somehow, was just a preparation for what was going to happen in the Valley.

I didn't know that, of course, until afterward. Most of

all I didn't know about the town of Winchester, which I think is the prettiest place in all the Valley. I didn't know about a little side street in that town, all grown up with big maples, with old-fashioned white houses half hidden behind them; or about one special house on that street, where a little schoolma'am named Lavinia Edwards lived with her crippled old father, thought her own thoughts, and kept quiet about them, while everybody else in town was thinking different thoughts and making a noise about them. I had never heard of Winchester and didn't know that a girl named Lavinia Edwards even existed, yet from the moment I hid a note to Uncle Ebenezer in the *Exposition of the Scriptures* and set out for Mr. Naylor's berry patch, I had really been going toward Winchester to find Lavinia. Because I did, all the rest of my life was different. And better.

So although Lavinia doesn't come into this story until a bit later I'll tell a little about her here, because everything that had been happening to me was just leading up to her. Also, she helped us win a very important battle—General Sheridan himself said so—which isn't a thing every schoolma'am does, in Virginia or anywhere else.

Old Dr. Edwards, her father, used to live in Ohio. A quiet, mild-mannered little man, he never made any trouble for anybody, yet he got into a good deal of trouble himself, ten years before the war, and his game leg was what he had to remember it by.

The way Lavinia told me, it happened like this.

Back around 1850 the state of Ohio was putting a turn-pike road through the town where she and her father lived. The contractors had brought in a whole bunch of

Irish laborers, who had made a rough sort of camp—
shacks, tents, and whatnot—a mile out of town. Because
they were making a long fill across a big marsh and had to
cut a way through a hill just beyond it, they were there for
a year or more but the townspeople didn't like them. They
liked the money the workers spent each payday, all right,
but they figured the men drank too much whiskey and got
into too many fights, and, besides, a lot of folks in that part
of the country just didn't like the Irish in those days.
Some of the workers had wives and families, but their
kids couldn't go to school in the town; nobody would have
anything to do with their wives, and the longer the camp
was there the worse the situation got.

Finally there was an epidemic of fever—the kind that
killed people. The townfolk said the fever came because
the camp was dirty and the workers were such heathens,
although I don't see what their being heathens could have
had to do with it—besides, they went to church when they
could find their kind of church to go to, which wasn't any
place near that little Ohio town.

As long as the fever was confined to the camp, nobody
in the town thought much about it, but it began to spread
to the town, so people grew angry and said the Irish ought
to be driven out. A delegation went to ask the governor of
the state to move them. Then the people figured that even
if the governor did something it would take a long time,
so there was a lot of talk about making up a posse and
driving the Irish into the next county. I don't know how
they thought the turnpike would ever get finished if they
did.

While all this was happening, Dr. Edwards went out

to the camp every day to look after some of the sick people there. The townspeople objected to this. Some of them told him he ought to stay in town and not treat any sick people but Americans (meaning the Irish road builders weren't Americans and never would be), but he paid no attention and kept on taking care of anybody who needed him. That was how he got mixed up in the trouble I mentioned.

Some woman in town—the wife of somebody important, I guess—got the fever and died of it. When word went around that she had died, a whole mob of men went out to burn up Irish-town. Dr. Edwards, who was treating some patients out there when the mob came, just went on with what he was doing, paying no attention to the warnings and the threats, so when the fight started he was in the middle of it.

He tried to go right on with his doctoring, even after the mob came charging in, just as if nothing mattered except himself and the sick people he was looking after, which might have worked except that the fighters were swarming in around the shacks, swinging clubs, firing pistols, and throwing things, and a brick hit him on the head and laid him out. Then the shack he was in got knocked over, he was half buried under the wreckage, and almost got burned alive when somebody set fire to it, but he was hauled out before the flames got him.

What happened to the doctor more or less sobered everybody, and the fight petered out with Irish-town only half destroyed. The mob went back to town, carrying the doctor and a couple of their own men who had been hurt, and nothing more was ever done about chasing the Irish out of the county. I guess in the end they even got the turnpike finished.

What Dr. Edwards got out of it was a bunged-up leg that was never much use to him after that, plus a low opinion of his fellow townspeople; when he was up and about again, after several weeks in bed, he quietly sold his practice and moved up to Winchester, in the Shenandoah Valley.

It wasn't really what happened to him personally that made him want to move. It was just that the whole business seemed so senseless, so ugly, that he felt he had to live somewhere else; it seemed to him that in some older part of the country things might be quieter, so he went to Virginia. In a few years the war caught up with him and went whirling right past his front door, a hundred times worse than anything the mob had done in Ohio.

But he did his best to live as if there wasn't any war, which was pretty hard because one army or the other was going in or out of Winchester all the time. He went his rounds and looked after sick people, and never talked about secession or abolition or the war itself if he could possibly help it.

Almost everybody else in town, of course, was strong for the Confederacy. Still, there were quite a few Quakers, Mennonites and Dunkers and the like there, so folks were used to men who did not believe in war. They liked Dr. Edwards, and never bothered him because he refused to support the Confederacy; he was sort of outside of the ordinary life of the town, and, except for his patients, hardly anyone came to call or to visit. I suppose he got pretty lonely.

The Girl in the Valley

Lavinia ought to have been lonely, too, but I don't think she was or ever will be. She was only fifteen when the war started, a grave little thing with quiet gray eyes and a way of looking a good deal more prim and demure than she intended; she never seemed to need to rely on anybody else to keep her company or cheer her up. She took care of her father and looked after the house with the help of Bonnie, a free colored woman the doctor had hired as cook and housekeeper. After the first year of the war she taught classes in a little school that had been organized after the regular men teachers had gone off to fight.

Lavinia was like her father in some ways and not like him in others. He didn't believe in the war, and tried to live as if it wasn't happening. But she was doing her own thinking, and after a year or two she concluded that even though she didn't really approve of the war, since it was going on anyway she had a right to hope that the northern side would win. So she hoped.

She never said anything to anybody about it. When, at different times, northern troops were in Winchester, and the local people would hardly give the boys the time of day, Lavinia didn't let on at all how she felt. She acted just the same as she did when the Confederate troops were in town; that is, she did her best to pay no attention at all. But all the while she was feeling stronger and stronger that the northern side was her side, and in the end that feeling was to make her do something very important to us.

That was still in the future, though. Meanwhile, she had her job teaching a class of children in the little private school not far from her house where she went every day, a tiny little thing in a gray dress with white collar and cuffs, and all of the things she thought she kept to herself. And all the while I was on my way to her, and I didn't know it.

13. THE FIGHT ON THE MOUNTAIN

It was a long road and a hard one. At the time, it seemed as if we were marching forever over the worst roads in the world, and when we weren't marching we were fighting battles that made Perryville look like a skirmish. As we marched, the army got lean and hard and self-reliant. I suppose I did, too, along with everybody else, although at the time I didn't realize that I was changing.

I still had bad moments. When Sheridan would swing into the saddle, nod to me to take the flag and ride after him, with the smoke and the racket and the killing just ahead of us, I would feel a cold lump in my chest, my mouth would be dry, and if I had to talk my voice would sound cracked and queer. I was learning that if you really have to do something you can make yourself do it, but it wasn't easy.

When Buell left the army we got General William S. Rosecrans in his place—a peppery, red-faced man with a big nose, very excitable and jumpy when there was fighting going on. After Christmas we set out after the Rebs, and ran into them on New Year's Day along a turnpike and in a cedar thicket beside Stone's River, near Murfrees-boro, Tennessee, and we had an awful two days' fight.

Perhaps that was the worst fight I saw in all the war, although all of them were bad and it's hard to say how one was much worse than any of the others. The Rebs almost licked us. They drove our line back two or three miles and nearly surrounded us. It was chiefly Sheridan and his division that kept them from actually doing it. Our division lost more than a third of its men but hung on to give Rosecrans and General Thomas and some of the others time to fix a new battle line and keep the army from being routed.

Sheridan himself was all over the place, as usual, and I was pelting along right behind him with that little flag. Long before the fight was over, I made up my mind that he and I and everybody around us were going to be killed for sure. It just didn't seem possible that anybody could keep on getting out of the places he kept getting us into.

The weather was cold and the place where we were fighting was mean and gloomy—lots and lots of scrubby, dark-looking evergreens set down in frozen fields, dead stalks of cotton that nobody had picked standing out in the open places. There was a woods they called "the round forest" where it seemed as if somebody had put all the guns in the world, and there was something about the clear cold air that day that made the sound of the guns especially loud. Some of the Rebs charging across those dead cotton fields actually stopped, picked wads of soft cotton, and stuffed them in their ears, the noise was so terrible.

We almost got licked, as I say, but in the end it was the

Rebs who retreated, and we moved on into Murfreesboro —where we stayed for six months afterward, as if it took the army that long to recover from the battle, which wasn't far from the truth. That summer we went on the march again, running Bragg and his army all the way back into northern Georgia. There our army got all spraddled out in the mountains and Bragg had a fine chance to pounce on us before we could get collected.

He didn't quite make it—that is, old Rosey got his army more or less pulled together before Bragg could bring on a fight—but in the battle that took place on Chickamauga Creek we got a bad whipping and had to hurry back to Chattanooga. Our retreat through the mountains at night after the battle is one of the things I don't like to remember.

I never saw Sheridan as glum. The Rebs broke our army in half, got in between the separated pieces, and the smaller of the two pieces got swept away and had to run for it. Sheridan's division was in the smaller piece, and although it wasn't our fault that the break had taken place we had to retreat along with everybody else. Sheridan was up and down the line of march, picking up fragments of scattered divisions and keeping things moving in some sort of order—swearing mad. He figured his division had been cut up and disgraced without having a fair chance to show what it could do, so he never had any use for General Rosecrans after that night.

We got back to Chattanooga and the Rebs came after us. They built trenches on a high mountain, Missionary Ridge, and looked down at us from the top of the ridge, waiting for us to get so starved we'd have to surrender.

We weren't exactly surrounded, but we couldn't use either the Tennessee River or the railroad to bring in supplies, and the only road was a miserable mule path that led for sixty miles through the mountains.

It was such a bad road, and the country was so barren, that it was almost impossible to use it to bring in anything for us to eat. The horses that pulled the wagons would starve to death unless most of the space in the wagons was used to carry their forage, and even then the army lost thousands of horses, whose dead bodies lined that awful road for miles and miles. We were so short of rations they had to put armed guards over the field corn that was kept for the cavalry and artillery horses. After the animals were fed, you could see soldiers hunting in the mud for stray grains of corn.

The Rebs really thought they had us, and for a while we thought so too. But the government called General Rosecrans back, just the way General Buell had been recalled a year earlier. Now the army was under General Thomas—"Pap" we called him. We all liked him and figured he would think up some way to get us out of our fix.

Then General Grant came to Chattanooga. He brought a lot of reinforcements and opened the supply lines so that we began to get plenty to eat again. We knew we couldn't be starved out now, and began to feel hopeful once more.

All the while the Rebs sat in their trenches on top of that long mountain wall, looking down at us. We knew that sooner or later we would have to drive them away, but it just didn't look possible, the ridge was so high and the Rebs had so many guns up there. Our own lines ran across a broad plain just outside of Chattanooga; it was as if we were on the stage of a theater and the Rebs were all up in the gallery.

When it came time for the battle, we were all keyed up. I never saw a fight where everything was so out in the open. All the way through, we had the feeling that everybody in the world was watching everything we did.

Up at one end of the line we had General Hooker and some troops he'd brought down from the Army of the Potomac, climbing over the shoulder of Lookout Mountain; 'way off at the other end of the line, General Sherman and his troops from down around Vicksburg were fighting their way across a chain of hills. In the middle Pap Thomas's army, with Sheridan's division in the front line, listened to the noise and waited for orders.

We were edgy. Hooker's and Sherman's soldiers had made a lot of cracks about the way we'd let the Rebs beat us—not knowing anything about what really happened, nor ever having licked anybody much themselves—and, now that the battle was on, Grant had given the big job to Sherman's men, as if he didn't trust Thomas's army.

When orders finally came late in the afternoon to advance and take the Confederate trenches at the foot of Missionary Ridge, everybody was keyed up. I saw something then that I never saw before or since: the cooks and hostlers and other extra-duty men, whose jobs excused them from fighting, were borrowing muskets and getting into the ranks with everybody else. Just that one time, we all really wanted to fight.

We set out across the plain, the high mountain wall straight in front of us extending far out on both sides.

All along the mountain the guns began to flash and sparkle, the smoke and noise came down, and it was like marching in the heart of a thunderstorm. A lot of our boys were hit, but we kept going.

Sheridan, his division formed in two lines, was riding Rienzi in the middle of the front line, and I was right behind him, carrying his flag—it had two stars on it now, for he had been promoted to major general that summer. When we got near the foot of the ridge, where the first Rebel trenches were, the boys gave a tremendous shout and broke into a run. Then we had the trench and the Johnnies were scampering up the slope to the main line at the top of the mountain.

We hadn't been ordered to do anything but take that first line—the one at the foot of the slope. But we couldn't stay there, because the Rebs on top of the mountain could shoot us easily. Anyhow all the boys were mad—at General Grant, at Sherman and Hooker and their soldiers, at the Rebs themselves, and at the way things had been going all fall—and we all figured that as soon as we'd caught our breath we were going to the top. All along the line I could see our boys staring up toward the crest, getting their wind in great big gulps with their mouths open, fairly twitching with eagerness as they built up their nerve.

I remember Sheridan sitting in the saddle, looking up to the crest. Straight ahead, at the summit, there was a Rebel battery whose gunners were training their pieces right on us. A Confederate officer was there, directing, and Sheridan looked straight at him. Sheridan pulled a silver flask out of his pocket, uncorked it, and suddenly

held it high in the air, gesturing toward that Confederate
officer that he was going to drink a toast to him.

He drank, the sunlight glinting on the silver flask, then
put the flask away. I saw the Confederate officer gesture to
his gun crews—and all four cannon went off at once. The
shots just missed us—we could feel the windage, and they
kicked up dirt and threw it in our faces—and Sheridan's
face turned dark.

"That's damned ungenerous!" he cried. "Just for that,
I'll take those guns!"

He looked along the lines beside him, swung his hat in
a big arc, then all of our boys jumped up and the whole
line started up the steep slope of Missionary Ridge.

How we got to the top I don't know.

The slope was long and steep—mounted men had to get
off and lead their horses—and the Rebs had a clear shot
at us all the way. They got a lot of the boys, but they
should have got all of us. Later on, we heard that when
General Grant saw us start the climb he said we would
all be butchered and swore he'd break the officer who told
us to go up.

But we did make it, and I think the Rebs got stage-
struck just watching us. That whole battle at Chattanooga
was too much out in the open. You could see everything. It
wasn't natural, and nobody acted naturally. I think if the
Rebs hadn't been able to see so much, they'd have licked
us. But we'd been coming on as if nothing could stop us
and finally the Johnnies began to think so themselves.
When the first of our boys broke over the crest of the
ridge, the whole Reb battle line went streaming off to the
rear.

So instead of a big fight when we got to the top we had a wild jamboree. We were all throwing our caps in the air, cheering and capering around like schoolboys. I remember Sheridan riding into the middle of the battery that had fired at him, jumping off his horse, and sitting straddle of one of the guns, swinging his sword and whooping.

I saw our old colonel, Gordon Granger, a corps commander now, riding along the ridge yelling at everybody: "You'll all be court-martialed! You'll all be court-martialed!" Between yells he would roar with laughter. Once I looked down into the plain and saw a cavalcade of horsemen with flags and banners coming over to see things for themselves—Grant and Thomas and their staffs.

When the generals got to the top we weren't there, for Sheridan did not give us much time to celebrate. He figured the thing to do was to keep crowding the Johnnies while they were still off balance, so he got his division into column and took it down the far side of Missionary Ridge, chasing the retreating Confederates.

He kept us on the road after the sun went down. Everybody was tired. We hadn't had a chance to boil coffee or eat supper, and a lot of the boys had lost their best friends on that mountain slope—even though we had come up fast, we lost a good many men before we reached the top—yet I never saw any soldiers who felt better than Sheridan's men felt that night.

We had worked off all our anger. If Chickamauga had disgraced us, the disgrace was wiped off the slate. We'd done a big thing, with Grant himself looking on, and Sherman's and Hooker's boys could wipe their eyes with it.

The Fight on the Mountain

We figured Pap Thomas had the best army there was and that Sheridan's division was the best part of Thomas's army. If Sheridan told us to keep going all night, we'd do it and be happy about it.

It got dark, and a big red-yellow moon came up, giving the hills and valleys that queer, unreal light things get in bright autumn moonlight where you can see just about as well as you can in the daylight, yet somehow nothing really looks quite the same, and the shadows are mysterious and silent.

Ahead of us there was a low hill, with some Rebs on it. Sheridan formed a battle line and opened fire, while he sent a couple of regiments around to the left to get on the northern end of the hill and flank the Johnnies out of there.

The moon was beyond the hill, and, when our two regiments went up, they were outlined against the light. The flash of their rifles looked pale and thin. It seemed as if the whole thing was being staged in a theater; certainly it didn't look like any battle I'd ever seen before. The Rebs ran away, leaving the road open again, and although it was nearly midnight Sheridan wanted to keep going.

Somewhere ahead there was a railroad. What was left of Bragg's army would have to use the railroad when it retreated. Sheridan figured we ought to grab that railroad to cut those Confederates off, but his orders didn't tell him to go that far; so he went galloping back to Missionary Ridge to see General Granger and get instructions—and reinforcements, too, if possible.

I rode with Sheridan, the little flag fluttering in the cool night wind, to Granger's cabin, and Sheridan went bus-

147

tling in, full of enthusiasm. He came out five minutes later, looking unhappy. Granger had gone to bed, and when Sheridan woke him up Granger said it was too late to do any more that night. Sheridan insisted, so finally Granger said he could keep going if he wanted to—if he ran into trouble, Granger would send another division to help.

We went back to where Sheridan's division was waiting, the men dozing by the roadside, and off we went again through that queer moonlight, skirmishers out in front. We came to a little river, which the skirmishers found was shallow enough to wade, but nobody knew how many Rebs there might be in the woods on the far side. It seemed to Sheridan that this was where he ought to have those reinforcements, but he wouldn't get them unless he was in trouble, so he decided to try a little trick.

He lined his men up in a broad battle line, facing the creek and the ghostly leafless woods on the far side, and ordered everybody to fire and to keep on firing. There was nothing to shoot at but the empty landscape, but back where Granger was the noise would sound like a battle, and maybe Granger would send another division forward.

There we were, lined up by a silent river at two in the morning, bright moonlight all around and not a sound in the night except the racket we were making. We fired volley after volley at nothing at all. Some of the boys thought the general was a little touched in the head but they were game to do whatever he said, so they kept on firing at nothing.

It was a weird, noisy, one-sided battle we had in the empty moonlight, shooting at nobody, nobody shooting back at us, and the long whacking volleys echoed back and forth over the river. The battle smoke went drifting up against the moon, making the queerest, eeriest, scariest sort of night I saw in all the war.

The trick didn't work. Granger heard us, but he knew the volleys were too regular for a real battle. He figured Sheridan was trying to fool him, so he rolled over and went back to sleep. Toward dawn Sheridan gave up and we stopped firing. The men went to sleep where they were, pickets out in front peering into the shadows looking for Rebs who weren't there.

So that was that. We might just as well have stayed back on Missionary Ridge with everybody else; we'd lost a lot of sleep, burned a lot of powder, and we hadn't accomplished anything. But that was Sheridan for you. He fought all of his battles that way—as if the whole war might be won then and there if we just kept at it hard enough.

14. SHERIDAN MOVES EAST

Since the war I have read all about our army's operations in eastern Tennessee, at the end of 1863 and in the winter of 1864. The books say we were doing a lot of marching and keeping a good deal busier than we usually were in the wintertime, but I don't seem to recall it that way. The three months after the Battle of Chattanooga, as I remember them, were a time when we were hungry, cold, and tired—they got us 'way off in the mountains, where the roads were so bad that not even Sheridan could always get his supply wagons through—but mostly it seems to have been a time of waiting. Perhaps that is because of the things that happened when spring came; things that were so new and different that, in my memory, they seem to cast their shadow in advance.

We'd had warning that there would be big changes, even though we didn't know what they would be.

After Chattanooga, everybody knew that Grant would be put in command of all the armies. Congress passed a law creating the rank of lieutenant general, which was a higher rank than anybody else in the U. S. Army held, and apparently the job was being made for Grant. Toward the end of the winter, we heard that Grant had been called to Washington. Then it was announced that he was Lieutenant General Grant—the top man of the whole war except of course for the President and the Secretary of War. He would stay in the east with the Army of the Potomac, and Sherman would command everything in the west. So we knew things were going to be different, but we still didn't know how it would affect us personally.

Then, one day in March, 1864, Sheridan got a telegram ordering him to Washington. On the heels of it came news that he was being put in charge of the cavalry of the Army of the Potomac.

So now he was back with the cavalry, where he had done his first fighting, and his infantry division was to have another commander. Nobody would go east with him except for a few staff officers. Then it was arranged that we enlisted men who were attached to his staff would move with him, bringing his horses and camp equipment and so on. That was a big piece of luck; he could easily have left us all behind and picked up new men in the east. I think he kept us because he wanted to have a few familiar faces around him for he hardly knew anybody in the eastern army.

Right after the general left, we got busy loading the headquarters stuff on freight cars. "We" were chiefly Joss Pettit, who was in charge, as tough and as crusty as ever, myself, and three privates. One of these privates was Otis Cleverdun because that winter one of the headquarters men got sick and was discharged. Before the vacancy was filled, I happened to be in the 2d Michigan's camp and looked up Otis.

He looked smaller and scrawnier than ever—army life hadn't filled him out any, the way it did with so many. He was brown as an Indian, and out of sorts, but very glad to see me.

"What's the matter, Otis?" I asked him.

"I wish I was back in Michigan," he said glumly.

"Who doesn't?" I shrugged.

"I'd like to see the logs coming down the river," he went on. "The ice won't be out yet, but it will be in another month and then they'll start the log drive. I'd like to smell the sawdust around the mill, and watch 'em loading lumber on the schooners. I'd like to go spearing suckers, down at Dare's pond. I'd like some of Pa's russet apples, out of a barrel that's been underground all winter. I'd like some buckwheat pancakes and maple sirup, and——"

Everybody talked like that now and then, thinking about all the good things he could see or do or eat if he wasn't in the army, but usually feeling that way didn't make a man look blue and grumpy the way Otis was looking.

"I'd like all that, too," I said. "But what's specially biting you? You feeling all right?"

He made a gesture with his hand as if he was tossing a pebble into the dirt. "Oh—sure, I'm feeling all right," he said. "But we don't do anything any more except guard wagon trains, or sit around blockhouses a hundred miles behind the lines, or ride out to pick up some Reb farmer's corn and pigs. The regiment's gone to pieces since Colonel Sheridan left." (Right to the end it was always Colonel Sheridan, as far as Otis was concerned.) "I wish I was out of it. I think maybe some day soon I'll *be* out of it."

I took a close look at him, and was worried. It wasn't hard to desert, even 'way down in Tennessee, if you really wanted to, and there wasn't a regiment in the army that hadn't had a number of desertions. But I didn't want Otis going that way; and just then I thought of that vacancy on the enlisted staff at headquarters. I knew Joss Pettit would pick the man, and since he wasn't riding me quite as hard now as he used to, I thought perhaps I could ask him a favor.

"You stay where you are," I told Otis. "I'll come see you later."

Then I hurried back to see Sergeant Pettit.

As far as I knew, Joss still thought that all cavalrymen who hadn't spent at least four years in the regular army were pretty no-account. I wasn't a bit sure what he'd say, but it was worth trying. So I went to him and asked to have my old pal Otis detailed to the vacancy on the headquarters staff.

Joss looked at me, with that sergeant's expression on his face that made you feel as if you'd forgotten to put your pants on when you got dressed, and said:

"Who is he, anyhow—another of these well-brought-up squirts who never said boo to a goose before I went to the trouble of teaching him which end of a horse you tie the nose bag onto?"

Then I got mad, good and mad, at the army and everybody in it, most of all at the noncoms who thought they ran the earth; and I blew up without caring much what happened afterward.

"I don't know if he ever booed at any geese," I exploded, "but I do know he walked fifty miles through the woods just to join your damned underfed cavalry in the first place. Since then he's made all the marches without falling out, been in all the battles without breaking for the rear, and he'll do a sight better than most of the stupid dog robbers you've got working for you. Also, I hiked fifty miles myself to join this army, and if I'd known ahead of time that pinning a sergeant's chevrons on some monkey's sleeves made him three times as big as the archangel Gabriel, I'd have stayed home and tried to amount to something, and if you don't——"

All of a sudden I ran out of steam, partly because I was so startled to hear myself talking that way to a sergeant, but mostly because of the expression that was coming over Joss Pettit's face. He was a little surprised and a little amused, and for a second I almost thought he was looking at me with something like admiration. Now he reached over and thumped me on the shoulder with his fist.

"Good man!" he crowed. "If this pal of yours has got as much spunk as you have, he ought to be all right. Give me his name. I'll put him on the detail."

That was how Otis got on the staff and went east with us.

It was early in April when our little string of freight cars was left on a siding at Brandy Station, in Virginia, and we got off to take our first look at the Army of the Potomac.

Everything was different here than in the west. There was a lot more style. You'd see a big group of horsemen jingling and clanking along, with fancy uniforms and polished metal, everything done just so. You'd think here was a crack cavalry squadron on its way to dress parade, but it would turn out to be some major general with his staff and a cavalry escort, no less, going off on some routine job. In camp the company streets looked as if they'd been laid out by engineers, they were so even and regular. They were particular about everybody having his uniform neat and clean, and his musket kept brightly polished. There was much more saluting, standing at attention, and saying "Yessir" than we'd ever been used to out west.

Army headquarters was showiest of all. General George Gordon Meade commanded the Army of the Potomac, and a red-and-gold banner the size of a tablecloth flew over his tent. All about there were other tents, snowy white and kept taut and smooth, with wooden floors and walls, laid out in streets like a regular little city. Meade had a cavalry escort, as dressed up and as dapper as so many West Pointers, a whole regiment, that kept its metal and leather so polished it fairly gleamed when the escort went trotting past.

"I'd like to see how those boys would look after a spell in the Mississippi mud," said Otis, first time we saw them.

Joss had been looking around, and he gave a little grunt.

"I bet there's plenty of mud right here when it rains," he said. "I wonder if those fellows ever do anything but wait on the general. I don't believe they'd be much in a fight."

Meade also had an infantry regiment at headquarters, and we'd never seen anything like it. They were Pennsylvanians, who wore what they called Zouave uniforms— big baggy red pants, with white gaiters on their ankles, yellow sashes around their waists, little blue jackets with red embroidery down the front, and yellow turbans instead of hats. They looked like home guards. We figured they couldn't keep those uniforms looking nice for five minutes if they ever really did any work, but folks told us they had done a lot of combat duty and were shot up pretty bad before Meade made headquarters guards out of them.

There was a headquarters band, too—a right good one, dressed in fancy Zouave uniforms just like the guards—that lined up by the general's tent every day at dinnertime, and again in the evening after retreat, and played for half an hour or so. All in all, even though we'd been in the army nearly three years, we began to feel for the first time what an impressive, showy thing a big army can be, and how much power and wealth must lie behind it.

Sheridan looked rather funny in all of this. The weather had burned his skin almost black, and he'd been so worn down he was underweight and skinny. His head looked too big and his arms looked too long. His uniforms never did fit very well anyway and his hat didn't fit at all. If it wasn't for the shoulder straps and his general air of authority, you'd have taken him for the sergeant of some wagon train who had wandered into headquarters by mistake. When he rode through, we could see the dressed-up eastern officers looking at him curiously.

Not that any of that worried Sheridan. He got right to work, and nobody on his staff—or anywhere in the cavalry corps, for that matter—got much rest from then on.

He had three divisions of cavalry—close to twelve thousand men, more cavalry than any of us had ever seen in one place before. He inspected every single regiment, and he inspected them hard—went through their stables, looked into cook shacks, talked with farriers and commissary officers, quartermasters and surgeons, in addition to watching them in maneuvers and on parade.

The men were in good shape, but their horses seemed to have been overworked and didn't look very well cared for. In the talks we had with some of the enlisted men, Joss and Otis and I found they were not in very good spirits. They claimed they'd never had a chance to show what they could do, and, while they didn't much like having an outsider from the west brought in and put over them, they were willing to overlook it if this new man would just do something with them.

"We spend all our time on picket duty," a big lanky sergeant complained, while a bunch of us were boiling coffee together after one of Sheridan's inspections. "We got a picket line sixty miles long around this army. All the time, we're either riding out to a picket post, doing duty after we get there, or riding back to camp again. No wonder our horses are played out. They never get any rest."

"How you going to take care of your horse when you're in the saddle twelve or fifteen hours every day?" demanded a red-haired little private.

"We never really *do* anything, with all that riding," said another man. "Infantry ought to picket its own camps. That ain't what cavalry is for."

"When we aren't on the picket lines we're escorting a wagon train up from Alexandria," the lanky sergeant spoke up again. "Either that, or else some infantry outfit has to go from here to there, and they make a couple cavalry regiments ride along in front just to see that they get there."

Joss blew in his coffee to cool it, and took a sip that sounded like a horse getting the last water out of the bottom of a bucket. Then he asked:

"What's the Johnnies' cavalry like, around here?"

"Tough," said the lanky sergeant. There was a general growl of agreement. "They use their cavalry right. They don't git all wore out riding picket. They keep it all in a bunch and hit us with it. Worst of it is, they know every road and cowpath and lane between the Blue Ridge and the Potomac. They always got the jump on us."

The redhead spoke up:

"That Jeb Stuart'll take all his cavalry over to our side of the river on a raid. He'll be across before we know he's moving. Then they call us together, and half of us got to ride thirty miles or more just to assemble. When we get assembled, we chase him. All the time we're *chasing* him. We never get around in front of him. Always following. So when the fight does come, our horses are all winded and his are fresh."

"And then," said the sergeant, sourly, "the newspapers all ask: 'What is our cavalry doing? Where is our cavalry?'"

Somebody damned the newspapers. The sergeant asked Joss:

"You got guerillas, out west?"

Joss nodded. "Bad. Especially in Tennessee. You got 'em here?"

The sergeant swore, kind of prayerfully.

"Yes. We got 'em here. The worst is a band led by a fellow named Mosby. They're all over. They knock you off

when you're on picket. They show up thirty miles behind
the lines and capture wagon trains and couriers. Once
they even caught a general. Went right into his house,
clear back near Washington, and took him out of bed and
rode off with him."

Guerillas were southerners who weren't really in the
army. They stayed home and tended their farms, but
they'd get together, now and then, with horses and guns,
sometimes in uniform—and ride around back of our lines,
raiding supply dumps, gobbling up stragglers, and doing
any harm they could think of. You could hardly ever catch
them because after the raid they'd disband, hide their
uniforms and weapons, and go back to working their
farms. The only people you could find would be innocent
farmers who'd swear up and down they didn't know anything about guerillas and you never could prove anything,
even when you knew they were lying.

Some of the guerillas were real mean. They'd sneak up
on a picket at night and cut his throat, and if they took
prisoners they'd kill them on the spot. Others were more
like regular soldiers and treated prisoners fairly decent.
But they were all pests, and our boys hated them. There
was more than one Tennessee farmer who'd got hung from
one of his own trees just because the boys suspected him
of being a guerilla. From what these soldiers said, I
gathered the same thing often happened in Virginia.

I don't know who Sheridan talked to, but he found out
what was bothering the cavalry and made a big change.
First of all, he got an order relieving the cavalry of all that
picket duty and pulling it together so it could be used the
way the Rebs used theirs. Then he bore down hard on

inspections. All of a sudden those cavalry horses began getting better care—lots more rest, better grooming, more to eat, better policing of the stables, and so on. Not long after that all sorts of new equipment began coming in, and the troopers who still had the old-fashioned single-shot carbines turned them in and drew repeaters.

After a few weeks of this, those Army of the Potomac cavalrymen began to feel better. It was the same with them as it had been with our Michigan cavalry regiment after Sheridan took charge. He was making men feel that they amounted to something, that what they were doing made sense, so of course they began to feel that he was great.

I noticed, riding at his heels on these trips around the camps, that now when he passed a cavalry camp and the boys down the company street spotted his little flag, they'd come boiling down to wave their caps and cheer. He made them proud of being cavalrymen once more. Without ever actually saying much about it, he got everybody feeling that this was the spring when Jeb Stuart's boys were going to get a licking.

There was just about a month of this, from first to last. Then very early one morning in May—a little after midnight, really—the headquarters staff was routed out to pack and saddle up. While the equipment was being stowed in the wagons, a bugler sent a thin, piercing call out into the darkness.

Other buglers picked it up and repeated it, until the night rang with it, and all through the cavalry camps there was a bustle and a stirring. In half an hour Sheridan went riding off down toward a crossing of the Rapidan River. In the night behind him where you couldn't see a thing you could hear a steady, unbroken, rustling noise, like a big river—twelve thousand horsemen, riding at a walk down the sandy roads that led to the river, starting out to open the last great campaign against Robert E. Lee's Confederate army.

15. I COULD FEEL MYSELF FALLING

Just below the Rapidan River, in the center of Virginia, there is a big stretch of woods they call the Wilderness, and it is the meanest piece of woods I ever saw.

I was used to woods of a different kind, back home. There we had forests running all the way from Lake Michigan to Lake Huron; great maples, and beeches, and miles and miles of white pines, trunks going straight up for fifty or sixty feet before they had any branches, floor clear of underbrush, everything almost like a park. There were lots of places in our woods where you could drive a team of horses and a wagon right through the middle of the forest, the trees were so spaced and the ground so clear.

There was always a soft green twilight in our woods; it was dim, even in the middle of the day, yet everything seemed to glow as if there was really plenty of light, only it was a little different from ordinary sunlight. It was always cool, and when you'd come to a stream it'd be clear as crystal, with cold water running over sand and pebbles and dead logs, and big trout lazying away in the pools or sliding up and down the riffles. I used to think those woods were about as much like heaven as anything I was ever likely to see.

But the Wilderness country was like the other place. It was all second-growth timber which had come in the way second-growth usually does—everything crowded and stunted, spiky little pines coming up through the slashing, with thickets of little saplings packed in so tight it was all you could do to force your way through. Even where the trees were big, the ground between was full of bushes, creepers, briars, and stubbly little growth that would never be any good to anybody. Here and there you'd find a little stream, usually at the bottom of a ravine, the banks covered with thickets and decayed logs, the water black and evil-looking, as if the sunlight never had a chance to touch it.

The country wasn't good for anything that I could see. There were just a few roads and hardly any farms; it was good land to stay out of, and it gave you the creeps just to go through it. As soon as our army crossed the river, it got into a terrible two-day battle with Lee's army right in the middle of all of this.

The cavalry was lucky. We ranged on ahead, down the narrow lanes that served for roads, and while we bumped the Rebs' patrols now and then we didn't have any serious fighting. The infantry got all of that, and how the infantry ever stood it I don't know because it was like fighting blindfolded. I heard infantrymen say afterward that in the whole battle they never saw any Johnnies—yet they were under close fire, and their regiments got all shot to pieces.

Out on the edges we could hear the noise of the battle.

It was an unbroken roar, which from a distance sounded a little like the surf on the beach during a big westerly gale —only it didn't really sound like that because you knew what was making the noise, what was happening to a lot of men who were in the middle of it, so it was frightening, and it hurt you to listen to it the way it never hurts to listen to a Lake Michigan storm.

Nobody really won that battle. The two armies just fought themselves out, and after resting for a day they sideslipped to the southeast to a little town called Spotsylvania Courthouse and started to fight all over again. On the way over there we had a grand mix-up.

Sheridan tried to get his cavalry to the courthouse first, to hold it until the infantry arrived. He did get one division there, but while he was bringing the others up Meade sent infantry along the road the troopers were using. Things got into such a tangle that before it was straightened out Sheridan's division was driven out of the town and the Rebs were in there to stay.

Sheridan blamed Meade and Meade blamed Sheridan, and they had a row that made the woods ring. I don't know what they said to each other, but I do know what came of it; because Grant, who finally got in on it, said that if Sheridan thought he could whip Jeb Stuart by taking all his cavalry and setting out after him the thing to do was to let him try it.

While the armies fought at Spotsylvania most of the cavalry was pulled back to the rear, where the men filled their cartridge boxes, packed rations and forage, and got ready to go. Sheridan had to leave some men to operate with the main army, but when he did get moving he had nine thousand mounted men, and he rode at the head of the column with nobody in front except a couple of squadrons to scout the way.

It was a fine thing to ride with Sheridan, carrying his flag, with that great big column of men coming along behind. I got the feeling that we had all the power in the world banked up on that road and that we were going to do something big with it. I felt that I had some of that power, myself; I wasn't a bewildered little straw-foot any more. I was a Somebody. I carried the flag, which was more than most of them would care to do. I was a real trooper —one of the men Phil Sheridan specially depended on. I felt good, that morning.

It was this trip that really showed the cavalrymen of the Army of the Potomac what their new general was like.

For one thing, Sheridan got everybody moving at a walk, just as he had at Booneville. In all their previous raids, these troopers had gone at a trot, pushing their horses hard—so they had always been worn out by the time they got into a fight. Now they went as if they had all the time in the world. Once in a while the column halted for a breather, everybody dismounting; there was no fuss and no hurry. If there was going to be a fight, both the men and the horses would be rested for it.

After we'd been on the road a few hours we heard firing up ahead, and the two advance squadrons came trotting back. Sheridan moved up the road to meet them.

"What's the matter, boys?" he called out, as they came back.

"Too many Johnnies up ahead," they explained.

"Cavalry or infantry?" asked Sheridan. They said all they had seen was Rebel cavalry.

Sheridan laughed and swung around in his saddle to look back at the long column behind him.

"Turn around, boys—we're going right on through!" he told the advance guard. "There isn't cavalry enough in the whole southern Confederacy to stop us!"

A couple of aides went spinning off with orders, and in a minute a brigade came trotting forward. It spread out into a fighting line. Sheridan swung his hat, his bugles blared, and the whole line surged forward, Sheridan in the middle of it. There was more firing, and the Rebs who had been blocking the road were driven off. In half an hour the long column was moving on as before, everybody at a walk, advance guard out in front—and every man in the corps had a new confidence in his ability to bust through any defense the Rebs might set up.

We got to Beaver Dam station, on a railroad line, that night, and set free several hundred Union prisoners who had been taken in the Wilderness and were on their way to the Richmond prison camps. Freight cars and warehouses were burned, and Sheridan said we'd destroyed three weeks' supply of food for Lee's army. After dark the fires glowed against the sky, the air was sharp with wood smoke and the tang of burned bacon, and the men went into bivouac.

The boys got another lift out of that. Usually, on a raid like this, half the men would be on the roads all night, picketing. This time just a few patrols were sent out, and everybody else turned in for a good night's sleep. Sheridan knew he had the jump on Jeb Stuart, and that nobody could bother us except a few scattered patrols. He never lost sight of the idea that if he was going to take his men into a fight, they mustn't get worn out first.

Next day we made another easy march, and at night we had a good camp in some rich meadows that gave plenty of pasturage for the horses. Otis went sauntering off through the camp after supper, and got back just as I was sliding into my blankets.

"You ought to hear the boys talking," he said, sitting down to take off his boots.

"What're they saying?" I asked. I was pretty sleepy and I didn't care much.

"They say they never been on a raid like this one," said Otis. "They say this is easier than staying in camp. They wish Sheridan had been here a couple years earlier."

"Wait till he gets 'em into a fight and then see how they like it," I said.

We had our fight next day.

We were just a few miles from Richmond now, near a little crossroads settlement called Yellow Tavern. Jeb Stuart had got his cavalry around in front of us—pushing his men night and day to make it—so in this fight, for a change, it was the Rebs who were all tired out at the start and our boys who were fresh. Sheridan's patrols tapped at the Confederate lines, then the men dismounted and Sheridan swung a long battle line in on the Rebel position.

It was a hard fight—those boys who told us that Stuart's men were tough certainly knew what they were talking about. There was a Rebel battery fixed so it could fire down the length of our line, and for a while the men wavered and seemed ready to fall back. But Sheridan had a mounted brigade in reserve—Michigan boys, led by little General Custer, who wore a fancy uniform and had perfumed yellow curls hanging down to his shoulders but who was a good fighting man just the same. This brigade charged the guns with sabers swinging, while the dismounted men rallied and then charged in on foot.

The field was full of smoke, the men were shouting, the guns were banging, and Sheridan galloped into the middle of things, swinging his hat, pulling his men along as if he was picking the battle line up in his hand. I was riding hard at his heels, gripping the staff of the battle flag, yelling my head off for no reason at all except that I was wild with excitement; it seemed as if Sheridan had a charmed life, the bullet that could hit him had never been molded. In all that noise and flurry I finally forgot to be scared and galloped along as if it were me, and not Sheridan, who commanded this army. . . .

And right then, of course, it happened.

Sheridan had just reined in Rienzi, the horse pulling up stiff-legged in a cloud of dust, flecks of foam on his black flanks. Shouting to a group of troopers, Sheridan told them the Rebs were beginning to run away, which was true. He swung toward the Rebel battle line, started forward, and of course I turned with him . . . and something hit me in the chest, hard. For a moment I had the silly idea that Sheridan himself had struck me with the flying fist that held his crumpled hat.

As I wobbled over, Big Red swerved and bumped into Rienzi, and I remember seeing Sheridan turn in the saddle. He reached out, took the flagstaff from my hand, then everything seemed to spin around and get blurry, and the battle noise sounded awfully far away. I could feel myself falling.

I came to in a field hospital, lying on the grass under a tree. A lot of others were lying around me, and a couple of surgeons and some orderlies were grouped around a sort of table. (They'd ripped the door off a cabin that stood near and laid it across a couple of stumps, to make an operating table.) There was a murmur of voices, and away off I could hear the battle. I didn't exactly hurt anywhere but I was awfully weak, and it seemed as if somebody had tied a rope around my chest too tight; I had the notion that I was swimming out in Lake Michigan; I could feel my strength going; my head dipped under the waves; I seemed to swallow a lot of water; I was choking and coughing; the water was warm and sickish-tasting in my mouth and throat, and I figured I was drowning.

Then I was lying on the table with the surgeon peering down at me, his white cover-all smeared with blood. I told him: "Please untie that rope!" and choked again. As he was opening my uniform, I sank under the waves once more.

I don't remember much about the next day or so. I know now that I was put in an ambulance and carried away, but all I can recall is being hot and uncomfortable, pumping and jouncing on the floor of the wagon. The dust in the air set me coughing, and whenever I coughed it seemed as if I was breaking in pieces. Finally, I was in a cot in a tent. The jouncing and the noise had stopped, the air wasn't so dusty, and I felt better; but I was so weak I thought I must be dying. I seemed to drift back and forth from waking to dreaming, and the dreams were so mixed up and disturbing that it was better to be awake than to be asleep.

Afterward, I found out this queer state lasted for days. I had been shot through the lungs and I had pneumonia. One of the hospital stewards told me later that the only reason he could think of why I didn't die was that I was too skinny.

"It's them big husky ones that go quickest," he said. "I don't know why it is. You skinny little fellers always seem to pull through even when you ain't supposed to." He sounded kind of aggrieved about it.

When I started to get better it seemed to happen all at once. I'd drifted off to sleep and was dreaming again; only this time the dreams weren't horrible as they'd been before. Everything was peaceful, I was walking down a shady street at twilight, and then I was facing a girl. She was little, with a proud way of holding herself, and she was looking at me with quiet gray eyes and saying: "I'm for the Union, and I'm the only one," which doesn't make much sense except that in the dream it seemed as if it did. When I woke up, thinking about her, the air was cool and pleasant, and somehow I knew I was going to get well.

I was in a hospital tent at Fort Monroe, where the wounded men from Sheridan's raid had been sent, and one day while I was lying there Joss Pettit walked into the tent.

I looked at him, surprised.

"The general told me to find out how you were," Joss said, in such a matter-of-fact way that it seemed the most natural thing in the world for a major general to be making inquiries about a wounded corporal. I guess that's because the major general was Sheridan.

"He told me to give you this." He held out an envelope, and when I opened it I pulled out two squares of blue flannel, with yellow stripes stitched to them. I blinked at them for a minute before I realized what they were—sergeant's chevrons.

"You're a sergeant now," said Joss. "The papers've gone through."

I tried to think of something appropriate to say but I was too overwhelmed. Instead I asked: "Who's carrying the general's flag?"

"Fellow from the 17th Pennsylvania named Weiderbach," he told me. "He's a big ox, all hands and feet. He's just on temporary detail. When you get well, you're to come back to the general's staff. He says you bring him good luck."

This was really good news. I still belonged to the 2d Michigan, and in the ordinary course of things when I left the hospital I would report back to my own regiment, which was 'way out west somewhere. Sheridan must have marked me as permanently assigned to his staff.

"You know what?" said Joss. "He don't like to have big troopers around him. I heard him say, one night by the campfire, that all the good cavalrymen are little fellows. He's little himself, of course. I think he likes to have you carry his flag because you aren't any bigger than he is.

And he knows he never has to worry that you'll lag behind."

For a minute it almost seemed as if the tent, my cot, and Joss himself were spinning around. I felt dizzy—dizzy, and happy, almost as if I wanted to bawl just because I felt so good. It didn't matter any more that I was a skinny runt— it never would matter again. I was Sheridan's kind of trooper, he was fixing it for me to come back to his staff, he'd sent his sergeant to see that I was getting along all right—and, by no means least of all, here was hard-boiled Joss Pettit sitting talking with me just as if I were a friend. Joss had as much as said that both he and Sheridan knew I was a brave man.

It finally occurred to me to ask: "Who won that fight?"

"The one where you got wounded? We did, of course. We licked 'em good. They took us front and rear one time, but Sheridan got us out of it and we made the Rebs hightail it. Oh yes—we killed Jeb Stuart, too."

"What happened to Big Red?" I asked then, feeling guilty, not having asked sooner.

"That little chestnut of yours?" said Joss. "He's all right. Funny thing—he insisted on trying to ride right behind Sheridan after you got hurt. I guess he figures that's where he belongs."

"I guess so," I said. I was sure glad nothing had happened to Red. I'd have missed him more than I'd have missed most people, but I only said: "Big Red is a dandy horse," and as I said it I felt like laughing, because I didn't need to call him *Big* Red any more. The size I was was the size Phil Sheridan thought was just right, and anybody who thought different could go run up a twig. This went for Red, too, as far as I was concerned.

"Yeah," agreed Joss. "He's a good horse. We got him in the headquarters string. He'll be there for you when you get back."

★

16. SHERIDAN'S NEW ARMY

It was early in August when I returned to duty. I was feeling pretty good, but still kind of weak, when I left the hospital at Fort Monroe for the big convalescent camp at Alexandria, across the river from Washington. I was only supposed to stay there for a day or so, but some clerk must have mislaid my papers because I was there for two weeks. That was good, because I picked up strength which I was going to need as soon as I got back on duty. I also picked up news about what had been going on in the army.

The Army of the Potomac was laying siege to Lee's army at Petersburg, below the James River twenty-five miles south of Richmond. Things were not going very well. Somehow the Rebs had scraped together another army and put it under a tough general named Jubal Early, who had come up across the Potomac and marched around in Maryland, coming close to capturing Washington itself. He'd gone back into Virginia, finally, but he was up in the Shenandoah Valley where he could easily get over into Maryland and Pennsylvania. The Army of the Potomac was never going to be able to beat Lee and take Richmond until someone took care of Early.

None of the Union generals seemed able to handle him, so Grant at last turned to Phil Sheridan. He sent Sheridan up to Harpers Ferry, which is where the Shenandoah River flows into the Potomac, and gave him a new army that was being assembled there. And when my papers came through I was ordered up to that place myself.

I fixed it so I could ride up on a freight train, and I got there about dusk. The town was such a little place I had no trouble finding headquarters, which had been set up in an old rat trap of a hotel. I went in and reported to the clerk in the adjutant's office—a private named Wade Meyers, who'd come east with us from Tennessee. After he'd checked my papers he stuck his head out a window and yelled for Joss Pettit.

Joss came in nonchalantly. He didn't act as if I'd been away at all—just asked: "You hungry?"

I was, and I said so. Joss took me back to the cook shack where I got a great big plate of beans, some hardtack, and coffee. Then he led me over to an old storeroom which the enlisted men at headquarters had taken over for a bunk-house. From somewhere they had got some cots and mattresses and even a few chairs and a table, and had the place fixed up snug as could be.

I sat down at the table and began to eat. The beans we used to get in the army were the best I ever ate anywhere because the cook would bury the bean pot in the coals overnight, and leave it there most of the next day, until the beans were all nutty and brown and sweet, swimming in molasses and melted pork. You could eat quarts of them without half trying—the only trouble was you couldn't cook them like that when the army was on the march.

These beans were right up to standard and I didn't bother to talk until the plate was half empty. After a while I looked up and just then in walked Otis and some of the other boys, and everybody wanted to know how I was feeling and what it was like in the hospital. Joss pointed with his thumb toward a big soldier I hadn't seen before and said:

"This is Ed Weiderbach, and he's one man who's really glad you're back."

Ed grinned, and I remembered Joss had said that he'd carried Sheridan's flag in my absence.

"Don't you like General Sheridan?" I asked him.

"I like him fine," said Ed. "But it just ain't healthy, carrying his flag."

"Be glad to get back to your regiment, hey, Ed?" asked somebody.

"I sure will. That Sheridan——" Ed shook his head. "I never *see* such a man. He's got a job that lets him stay back in the rear where things is quiet. But does he stay there? Not him. He's up front *all* the time. He isn't happy unless a lot of people are shooting at him."

Ed shook his head again and we all laughed. Somebody said maybe Sheridan would be different, now that he was in command of a whole army, but nobody really thought so. He just wouldn't be Sheridan unless he was storming around where the shooting was going on, and we all knew it.

"So he's got an army of his own now," I said. Otis said:

"Yep," and Joss added: "If you can call what he's got now an army."

"What's the matter with it?" I wanted to know.

"Well, it was just sort of throwed together," Joss snorted. "And most of the men in it aren't much good."

"Them Sixth Corps boys are all right," somebody objected.

The Sixth Corps was out of the Army of the Potomac, and supposed to be one of the best outfits there was anywhere.

"Yes, they're all right," said Joss. "But they been shot up pretty bad, and they're awful low-spirited right now. They were in that fight at Washington, and since then they've had the legs marched off of them. Now they're 'way down. They don't keep their camps policed good and they don't keep their muskets clean. They act like they're pretty sick of the war."

Somebody muttered: "Don't blame 'em much," and another man said the Sixth Corps hadn't acted like itself since Cold Harbor. That was a fight that happened after I'd been wounded which they said was about the worst the army ever had.

"Who else is there?" I asked.

"Well, there's some boys from what they call the Nineteenth Corps," said Joss. "They been down in Louisiana all the war. They never did much fighting down there, but they say the weather was always hot and sticky and they look sort of thin and brown and washed out. Then there's a bunch of regiments in the Eighth Corps. They been up here in the Valley or over in the mountains west of here ever since the war started. They got licked every time they ever had a fight."

He shook his head in slow wonder.

"I don't know how it is, but those boys *always* get licked," he mused. "They just don't seem to amount to anything at all."

Otis said confidently: "Sheridan'll fix 'em up." I thought so, too, but I had to admit the layout didn't look very good. I asked: "What cavalry is there up here?"

Joss looked brighter.

"Cavalry's all right," he said. "We got two divisions of Sheridan's old cavalry from the Army of the Potomac—Torbert's and Wilson's—and General Averell has got a little division of cavalry from over in West Virginia. Altogether, I suppose we got about nine thousand cavalry. But, Lord!" He began wadding tobacco into a curved briar pipe. "You can't make a campaign with just cavalry. This Early, now, he's got a lot of infantry right out of Lee's army. Those boys are tough."

He lit his pipe and puffed a moment in silence.

"Another thing," he said suddenly, taking the pipe out of his mouth and jabbing at me with the moist stem, "they got guerillas up here in the Valley worse than any you ever heard of. Don't you ever wander off outside the lines alone. They'll get you if you do. And they mean business. They don't ever take prisoners. They just shoot you, or cut your throat, soon as they catch you."

"Mosby's men?" I asked.

"Yeah. Mosby's, and a lot of others, too. Thicker'n fleas on a dog's back. And *mean*, I tell you."

178

Somebody said: "The boys sure don't like guerillas." Another man spoke up:

"When we move up the Valley, if you see a body hanging from a tree anywhere, you'll know the cavalry's caught another guerilla."

As it happened, we started to move up the Valley the next day, heading southwest to Winchester, which was twenty-five miles away.

It wasn't bad marching. The weather here was cooler than down in southern Virginia, the roads were a lot better, and there was something about having the mountains lying blue and hazy on the sky line, about seeing the solid farmhouses with their big barns and their well-tended fields, that made everybody feel good—as if maybe the war wasn't going to last forever, after all, and some day people could really start living again.

As we moved, Sheridan was all up and down the column. First he'd be up front with the cavalry patrols, to see how they were doing. Then he'd be back with the infantry, seeing that the line of march wasn't held up and that every unit was where it was supposed to be. Once in a while there'd be a tie-up, just as there always is on the line of march—an artillery caisson would lose a wheel, or a culvert would collapse, or a wagon train would come lumbering across a road an infantry division was trying to use—and the minute that happened Sheridan was certain to come riding up to straighten things out.

He'd go back among the supply trains, too, and if these fell behind or took the wrong road, the officer in charge would hear about it right off, in a way he wouldn't forget. Sheridan would come up through the artillery columns, then go skimming up front again, and, in between these moves, he'd cast off to the side to see how the flank guards were doing their job. He probably traveled three times as far as the rest of the army. And so did his color bearer.

The point is that this made things easier for the men in the ranks. A march that runs smoothly isn't half as tiring as one that gets tangled. You can make camp in the evening before dark, and after supper there's time to sit around, have a smoke, and visit a little before crawling into the blankets. Also, when the wagon trains move right, everybody gets his rations on time.

It wasn't long before the army began to show the difference. The sallow, underweight boys in the Nineteenth Corps began to look more chipper, and when Sheridan rode past they'd swing their caps and give him a cheer. Even the boys in the Eighth Corps, who had been licked every fight they'd ever had, perked up and began to look like soldiers instead of like men who'd got lost from a militia muster. Only the Sixth Corps stayed glum.

Actually, the Sixth Corps people were beginning to like Sheridan. You could tell that, talking with them. But they'd been in the army a long time and they'd been in all of the big battles. They'd seen generals come and they'd seen them go, and they just weren't the cheering kind any more. They knew things were going better, now Sheridan was in command, and they liked him for it. But they knew, too, that sooner or later there'd be a great big fight in which they would have to do most of the fighting, and they just didn't have much enthusiasm left. What little they did have, they weren't going to waste cheering.

One morning near Winchester, where the army was

waiting a day or so while the cavalry scouted around, I'd been down giving Big Red a grooming—Sheridan didn't much care how we kept our uniforms, but we sure had to keep our horses looking good—when I ran into Otis and Ed Weiderbach. I just stopped and gaped. Both of them were wearing Confederate uniforms.

Not that the Rebs were ever very particular about uniforms—in a lot of cases they didn't have much uniform to be particular about. A Reb soldier might wear anything at all, from homespun pants and shirt to a faded blue coat taken from some Yank, but mostly they were able to wear some sort of outfit that at least showed they were Confederate soldiers.

Anyhow, here were Otis and Ed, togged out in gray pants that had seen a lot of wear and butternut-brown shirts like so many of the Johnnies wore. They had tattered, greasy black slouch hats on their heads, carried Reb equipment, and looked exactly like a couple of hard-riding Confederate cavalrymen.

"What on earth are you boys up to?" I asked.

Ed grinned a sheepish kind of grin and pushed his old hat farther over on the side of his head. Otis tried to look important.

"We're Sheridan's scouts."

"*Scouts?*" I was startled.

There was a big difference between going out scouting and being what was called a scout. Lots of soldiers went out on scouting expeditions, but they never called themselves scouts. A scout was a spy, going round behind the Rebel lines in Rebel clothes. If he got caught by the enemy, he was sure to be hanged right away. Most soldiers wanted no part of that sort of thing. But here were Otis and Ed, dressed up like Johnnies and calling themselves scouts. It didn't make sense.

"The general has a new idea," said Otis, still important, as if he and Sheridan had sat down together to plan things. "He's recruiting a whole company of scouts to handle the guerillas. The guerillas wear our uniforms half the time, so we're going to wear theirs and fool 'em. Also, we'll pick up all kinds of information for the general."

As an afterthought, he added: "Major Young of the 2d Rhode Island is in charge of us."

"You mean you're going to ride around the country togged out like that?" I asked. Otis and Ed nodded.

"The Rebs'll hang you sure if they catch you," I pointed out. "And if they don't, how're you going to keep our own pickets from shooting you when you come back?"

"We'll be all right," said Otis. "Major Young has got it all worked out."

Otis wasn't much bigger than a tadpole, but right now he looked as if he figured he was the most important soldier in the army. I looked at Ed, who was still grinning. A shock of sandy hair was sticking out through a hole in his hat, a couple of toes were poking out of one of his boots, and I had to admit he looked like a Johnny—a Johnny who had seen better days.

"I thought you figured carrying Sheridan's flag was too dangerous," I said. "Can't you see that this job is going to be about five times as risky as any battle?"

"It's different," argued Ed. "I don't mind taking chances when I'm on my own. It's riding straight into the firing with that little flagstaff in my hand that gets me. You can't shoot back and you can't run away. All you can do is follow big Rienzi's rump and hope nothing hits you. I'd rather go scouting."

He pulled a plug of tobacco out of his pocket and bit off a big hunk.

"Besides," he said, "we get chances to do a lot of foraging, this way."

I could see his point. All of our boys figured that anything they could pick up in the way of food on a Rebel farmer's place was fair game. While it was supposed to be against the rules, it was more or less expected that they'd bring back a pig or a few chickens when they had a chance. But some of them really developed taking ways and would lift any sort of valuables—watches, money, whatever they could lay their hands on—whenever they could. That was just plain robbery, of course, and if the man who had been robbed could get into camp and identify the men who had robbed him, they'd be in plenty of trouble. But if the farmer thought that the men who robbed him were Confederates, he'd never have a chance to catch up with them. They could do anything they wanted to.

"One way or another, both of you will get hung before this is over," I prophesied grimly.

Otis shook his head and repeated: "We'll be all right." Ed just winked at me and said: "It beats carrying the flag."

I soon found out that Otis had told a straight story, only he hadn't told half of it. Major Young had close to a hundred men in his company of scouts—mostly wild young daredevils who didn't care much what happened to them so long as they had a little excitement. They spent most of their time in Confederate uniforms, roaming about the country in little groups, tracking down guerilla bands, finding out where Early's army was, spreading false news about Sheridan's movements—and, on the side, having a high old time for themselves.

They did so much foraging, and broke so many rules doing it, that the rest of the boys called them "Sheridan's robbers." I heard an officer once speak of Major Young and his command as "Ali Baba and his forty thieves." Quite a few of these scouts did get killed, in the end. The rest of them had fun.

17. A LETTER FROM LAVINIA

For a few days the army was near Winchester. Sheridan had his headquarters in the town, and evenings we used to stroll around to see what we could see.

The town was nice enough, with big houses and shady streets, but I felt like an outsider there. The people had no use at all for Union soldiers. There were lots of girls, and they were awfully pretty—we'd been in army camps for so long, with nobody to talk to or look at except other soldiers, that these girls in their clean dresses looked like the sweetest, daintiest people that ever lived—but they didn't give us a bit of their time.

A couple of us would be sauntering along and we'd see some girls coming, but before they reached us they'd cross the street, carefully looking away from us. Sometimes, they'd walk straight by us holding their handkerchiefs up to their noses, looking to one side and frowning as if they'd got a whiff of something terrible; or if they looked at us, by accident, they'd make faces, and say things to each other about "Yankee scum." Once I heard one girl say something about "foreign mercenaries from the city slums."

I wanted to talk back to them and tell them I was a volunteer, that I'd been born in this country, and even though Winchester wasn't a very big place it was a lot bigger than any town I'd ever lived in. But somehow I never said anything.

It made me wonder, though. We might have been having a good time, walking along in the dusk, talking things over, maybe stopping in somewhere for a little ice cream, or sitting on the porch in the twilight while somebody inside the house played the piano, the way young folks do in other places. It ought to've been that way; we'd been born in the same country, we talked the same language, we were the same age, and all of us were kind of lonely.

But, no—we were enemies. We couldn't speak to each other. They made faces at us and dropped hard remarks where we could hear, and in the next fight those girls would all be hoping we'd get hurt, while we'd probably be doing our best to hurt their brothers or sweethearts. When such thoughts came to me, war seemed really terrible, not just because a lot of people got killed but because it cut folks off from each other, made them hate when there didn't seem to be any real reason for it.

One hot afternoon I had to ride southwest of town to take a dispatch to some infantry outpost. The road was stony and covered with dust, and on the way back Red lost a shoe and went lame, so I got off and walked along leading him. I came into town through a side street, along toward evening, dusty and out of sorts, and went stumping along with the reins in my hand, Red clumping behind me, neither of us very happy.

Then I heard a girl's voice saying:

"Soldier, are you thirsty?"

There were trees on both sides of the street, and packed earth sidewalks. On the right, where this voice was coming from, there was a white picket fence, with shrubs behind it and a trim white house with green shutters off beyond. A girl was standing by an open gate in the fence, one hand on the gatepost—the first person in all Winchester who had ever said a friendly word to me.

I stopped and stared at her. She was little and slim, very neat in a gray dress with white cuffs and a little white collar, standing in a proud, erect way as she looked at me. She wasn't scowling or making faces, and she wasn't being too easy and friendly either, the way some girls were in some towns. She was grave and serious, and looked as if she was sorry for anyone who had to be hot and tired and dusty. Somehow it seemed the most natural thing in the world for a Virginia girl to ask a Union soldier if he was thirsty.

"Yes, ma'am, I am," I said finally. "Could I have a glass of water, please?"

"Of course." She looked at Red, and then added: "I expect your horse must be thirsty, too, isn't he?"

"Ma'am, he sure is," I said.

"Bring him back here." She swung the gate farther open.

So the next thing I knew, Red and I were crossing the lawn and following her around to the back, where there was a little carriage house without any carriage in it, standing there with its doors propped open. In front of the carriage house there was a wooden pump, with a big bucket under the spout. She pointed to it.

"If you want to pump some water for him from the cistern, I'll get some spring water for you. It's colder and it tastes better."

Then she slipped off and went in the kitchen door, while I began to work the creaking pump handle. I had a notion to call after her and say that the water from the cistern would probably be five times as fresh and sweet and cold as most of the water we'd been getting these last two or three years, but I didn't. I filled the bucket and set it under Red's nose. While he was drinking she came back with a little tray carrying a blue earthenware pitcher and a glass. I poured out a glass of water and drank it. Then I set the glass back on the tray and looked at her.

"Thanks, ma'am," I said. I wanted to keep on talking, but I couldn't seem to think of anything to say. Red got down to the bottom of the bucket and made a long sucking sound, and I heard myself saying:

"I like to see horses drink. They always act as if they enjoyed it so much."

She said: "You forgot to say 'ma'am.'" I quickly added "ma'am," and then saw she was smiling. I could feel myself blushing, but it wasn't a mean smile, as if she was laughing *at* me, so I had to smile, too.

"I'm not used to talking to girls," I explained. "You're the first Sesesch girl in Virginia that's even said hello to me."

Her smile faded.

"I'm not Sesesch," she said quietly. "I'm for the Union. But I suppose I'm pretty nearly the only one in Winchester."

It seemed as if all of this had happened before, some way. Maybe I had dreamed it, or maybe she was just my

kind of folks; I didn't know, but all of a sudden I didn't
feel shy or awkward any more. Then I remembered I had
a message to take back to headquarters. I was going to be
late with it anyway because Red had gone lame, and it
wouldn't do to stand here any longer. More than anything
else I wanted to see her again, so I asked:

"If I come back here after supper, could I see you?"

She had nice gray eyes, and she looked at me very seriously as if she was thinking it over. I said: "Ma'am?" real
quick, as if I'd forgotten it again, and she laughed.

"Of course you can, if you want to," she said warmly.
Then I thought of something else, and it worried me.

"Everybody else in town is Reb," I said—as if she didn't
already know it. "Would it be all right? I mean, will the
neighbors talk, or be mean, or anything, if you let a Union
soldier come to call on you?"

"They'll talk, of course, but it doesn't make any difference. Besides, they've already seen you. What's your
name?"

I told her. She said: "My name's Lavinia Edwards. My
father is a doctor here. If you want to come by this evening, we'll be glad to have you."

I went back to headquarters feeling pretty good. I de-
livered my dispatch and took Red down to the blacksmith's hut for a shoe. After supper I got a couple of
buckets of water, stripped, and washed off all the dust and
sweat that was sticking to me. Then I freshened up my
uniform as best I could and got dressed. Joss and a couple
of the others watched me and made remarks, because they
knew nobody in his senses would bother doing what I
was doing unless he had found a girl to call on.

"Watch out for these Sesesch girls," Joss warned. "They'll lead you on and then turn you over to the guerillas."

"Yeah," said somebody else. "We'll look for you in a ditch outside of town tomorrow morning. With your throat slit."

"She's not Sesesch!" I said. I didn't want to be talking about her at all, but I didn't want anybody to think I was going calling on a Reb. "She's for the Union, all the way."

A familiar voice said: "You sure about that?"

I looked up and there was Sheridan, standing with his thumbs hooked in his belt. He was always stalking around the headquarters layout, and it wasn't at all unusual for him to stop and talk with some of the boys.

I said: "Yes, sir. I'm dead sure." I'd only talked to her for a minute and I didn't know a thing about her, yet somehow I was sure. I remembered how it was, looking into her eyes, and I knew—as well as I'd ever known anything— that you could believe anything she ever said or did or was.

Sheridan grinned. Then, as he turned to go, he jerked his head and said: "Come over here, Sergeant. I want to talk to you."

I followed him, and in front of the headquarters tent fly he stopped.

"You're sure about this girl?" he asked again. I said: "Yes, sir, I am."

"Nice girl, is she?"

"Yes, sir. She's Dr. Edwards's daughter."

"You going to her house?"

"Yes, sir."

"One of these days," said the general slowly, "we'll probably go away from here. When we do, it's important for us to know somebody in this town who's on our side and can give us a little news if we need it. When you come back here tonight, I want you to let me know whether she'd be willing—if you slipped back to see her after we've moved out—to give you a little note for me, telling me anything she can about what the Rebels are doing."

He stopped, and I blinked at him. He was awfully casual about me slipping back into town after we'd left. That would be a risky job. Yet what he said was making my pulse beat faster, not because it scared me but because it meant I would be able to see her again even after the army moved away.

"What I want, mostly, is news of Rebel troop movements," Sheridan explained. "If they get reinforcements, I need to know that. Even more, I need to know when they send any of their men back to Richmond. One of these days they'll be doing that, and when they do I've got to know. Find out if she can do that for us."

He turned to go into his quarters, but just before he went he grinned again and said: "Make awfully sure you're not being fooled." Then he was gone, and I was on my way.

I walked, because the house wasn't more than half a mile away. When I turned in at the gate and went up the walk it all seemed familiar and natural, as if Lavinia was somebody I'd known all my life. Dusk had come down, the white front of the house seemed to float up out of the shadows as if it was unreal, the shutters had been closed so there wasn't a light to be seen, and under the porch roof it was dark as a cave. Then her voice said "Hello," and I could hear the chains of a porch swing creak as she got up and walked over to greet me.

We shook hands. Her hand felt tiny but strong, as if it was a hand that did plenty of work and was good at it. When she opened the front door, yellow lamplight spilled out into the darkness, and she led me into a pleasant, high-ceilinged room where Dr. Edwards was sitting in a rocker.

He was friendly: a little over medium height, I judged, and thin, with kindly eyes and a sort of sad, gentle look about the mouth. I thought of him, at the time, as an old man, although I know now that he wasn't old. The room was sort of shabby but comfortable, as if the people who lived in it liked it and felt very much at home in it; and I felt as if I had reached a safe, homelike place that I had been looking for a long time.

When they asked me questions I leaned back comfortably and talked, and before long I was telling them all about the town where I lived: about Uncle Ebenezer, his store and his house, about the sawmill, the log drives, and the lumber schooners, and about how I had run away from home to enlist. The doctor sat with one elbow on the arm of his chair, rubbing his chin with a thumb and forefinger, and asked little questions that kept me going. But he didn't seem to be prying: it was more as if he was someone I had known when I was small who had gone away and was just getting brought up to date on the home-town news. Lavinia sat on a couch with her feet tucked up out of sight under her skirt. Finally she asked:

"Do you want to go home very much?"

I thought about Uncle Ebenezer. We'd written to each other quite a few times in the last year, and I knew he wasn't angry any more. Still, it wasn't exactly to see Uncle Ebenezer that I wanted to get back. I wanted to see if the woods and the water and the clean air still looked and smelled the way they used to. I wanted to know what it was like, once more, to loll on top of the Lake Michigan bluff and watch the west wind bringing in a schooner. I wanted the old feeling of excitement that used to come to me when I thought about making my own way in the world; only it seemed now as if the world I wanted to make my way in was the familiar world back home instead of the unknown world that lay off beyond the horizon.

"Yes, I do," I said. "But I don't want to go back to everything just as it used to be. I want things to be different. For me, I mean."

What I really meant was that I wanted to go back as the man I had become, not as the boy I had been, but I wasn't saying it right and I felt embarrassed. But she wasn't laughing at me. She said:

"After all, that's what you're fighting for, isn't it—to make things different?"

I hadn't thought about it that way before, and I wasn't sure she was right.

"Well," I said, "we're fighting for the Union."

"And for freedom, too, aren't you?"

"I guess so. Yes, of course." We never talked about it that way in camp. All we ever said was that we couldn't go home until we'd licked the Johnnies.

"Well," she countered, "won't that make everything different?"

I was doubtful.

"Maybe so," I said. "But we want most things to be the

way they used to be. We don't want everything different. We want it like it was."

Dr. Edwards looked unhappy, as if he had to break some unpleasant news.

"The only trouble," he said, "is that that's the one thing we can't possibly have."

He smiled as if he was apologizing for something, and then went on:

"We fight wars to keep things from changing, but the wars make change certain. They begin just because people are angry and impatient, but they collect ideas as they go along. Our war has collected the ideas of unity and freedom and a great many things will eventually be very different."

He paused; and then said:

"Take your General Sheridan, for instance. Why do you suppose he is fighting?"

"Why," I said, "General Sheridan just *likes* to fight."

Dr. Edwards smiled.

"I have no doubt of that," he said. "But I don't think General Sheridan wants everything to be just the way it used to be.

"You see, General Sheridan is Irish. His father came to this country—thirty or forty years ago, I suppose—to make a living digging ditches. So did many other Irish. They've built most of our canals and highways and railroads since then.

"We've never really welcomed them. They talk with a brogue, most of them are poor and ignorant, and their ways are not like ours. They go to a different church. Their racial memories and family backgrounds aren't like ours.

"So we've made outsiders of them. We've used violence to keep them from becoming real Americans—and at the same time we complain because they aren't real Americans."

He stopped, and I waited for him to go on. He made a little gesture with his hands.

"Enforce unity between North and South," he said, "and sooner or later there has to be unity between native-born Americans and immigrant Americans; between lucky Americans and unlucky Americans; between people whose ancestors came over on the *Mayflower* and people whose fathers came over on a plague-ridden packet ship from Dublin or Hamburg or Trieste. Make colored men free, and sooner or later *all* of us will be free. And nothing at all will be the same as it used to be."

He thumped his palms against the arms of his chair and sat up straighter, as if to dismiss the subject.

"The war hardly meant that when it began," he said. "Now it cannot mean anything else. Men have not fought for a nobler ideal. I envy you the privilege."

Since the war had begun, lots of people had said that they envied us soldiers the privilege of fighting for the Union, but most of the people who talked that way took good care not to get into any of the fighting themselves. We had plenty of names for people like that, in camp, and often invented new ones. But with Dr. Edwards it was different: he really seemed to make sense, somehow.

"Lavinia," he said, breaking the silence that followed his last remark, "isn't there some lemonade in the kitchen?"

She went and got it—a big pitcher, all beaded with moisture, with ice clinking in it—and she also brought in a plate of pound cake, and the two together seemed to be better than anything I had ever eaten. While I was eating the cake I remembered what General Sheridan had said, and told her about it, asking if she would do what he wanted.

"Of course," she said, after a moment's thought. "I don't know if it will do very much good. Sometimes we hear things, though."

Then she looked at me, her eyes serious.

"You'll come and get the letter?" she asked.

I nodded. She looked at her father, then looked at me again, and seemed worried.

"You mean you'll come to get it after the Union army has moved away and the Confederate army is here?"

I nodded again.

"That'll be awfully dangerous for you," she said. "You don't know how carefully they patrol the streets and the roads. If they caught you——"

In the old days I probably would have swelled out my chest and told her that of course it would be terribly dangerous but that I was a brave soldier who wasn't afraid of anything and rather enjoyed taking long chances. But I didn't feel like doing that, with her. I certainly wanted her to like me, but I didn't want her to like me for something that wasn't really so. Anyway, it seemed as if I didn't need to pretend any more. So I just said:

"Oh, General Sheridan will find a way to get me through all right."

She stood up, and I knew the evening was over. She

came over, took my hand, and gave it a firm, friendly little shake.

"Goodbye, Bob—it's a bargain," she said. "I'll write the letter if you'll come and get it."

18. A NIGHT RIDE TO WINCHESTER

A few days later the army marched south. We stopped at Strasburg, a little more than twenty miles from Winchester, while Sheridan's scouts and cavalry prowled about to see what General Early and his army might be up to.

Sheridan was being cautious, and it didn't seem natural. From campfire talk we heard that he was under strict orders to take no chances. The war was not going well, a presidential election was coming, and if Sheridan's army got licked the government figured people might get so discouraged they'd want to quit. I don't know whether that really would have happened, but that's what everybody was afraid of; and after we'd been around Strasburg a few days Grant sent orders for Sheridan to go back to the neighborhood of Harpers Ferry and wait for a break.

I don't like to think about that retreat. We had just begun to feel that things were going right—and here we were, running away from a fight. It reminded me of the old days in Mississippi, when the army marched around in circles all the time without getting anywhere. Besides, we had a mean job to do on the way back.

A Night Ride to Winchester

All through the war the Rebs had got supplies from the Shenandoah Valley. It was good farming country, and its wheat and corn and meat had been feeding Confederate armies for years. When they crossed the Potomac, the way Early had done in July, they never had to worry much about rations—they could get all they needed right there in the Valley.

When Sheridan retreated, Grant ordered him to burn out the whole Valley so that the Rebs could never get any more food there. As we marched toward the Potomac the cavalry in the rear spread out from mountain to mountain, driving off herds of cattle, loading wagons with grain, burning barns and haystacks and corncribs, and leaving the country black and desolate.

It wasn't nice to watch. Sheridan's orders were to leave the farmers enough food to get them through the fall and winter, but that was hard to figure and there were a lot of characters in our cavalry who took to this burning and destroying business with a little too much enthusiasm.

It was hard for a family to see everything it had worked and saved for going up in smoke. Some of the people stormed and raged and cried, and acted as if they would hate us forever. Others seemed dazed and stood by in silence, while our cavalry turned them into paupers. Day after day the big columns of black smoke would go up, all across the Valley, and at night you could see the flames and the glowing embers for miles: it was beautiful, until you stopped to think about it, and then it looked ugly. If I had ever thought that war was gay and romantic, I stopped thinking so on that march down the Valley.

Finally we got to our old camping grounds near Harpers

Ferry, and went into bivouac there and waited. Sheridan was impatient; you could see that, the way he stalked around headquarters, glowering. He wanted to pitch in and fight, but was strictly ordered not to do that until he was sure he could win, and he couldn't be sure of that until Early sent some of his troops back to Richmond.

Sheridan's scouts were busy. They put on their Confederate uniforms and rode off every which way, looking for the information Sheridan needed—but they didn't get it just then.

The guerillas were busy, too. The burning and destroying we had done had them all worked up, and they swarmed around like mosquitoes. Now and then one of our scouts or couriers would be missing, and a day or so later we'd find the dead body by a roadside. Then the scouts would go out to get revenge, and they weren't particular about where or how they got it. They just got it.

I could see a change coming over Otis. He had always been mild, happy-go-lucky; now he was getting hard, and it bothered me. One night he came by the campfire where Joss and I were sitting, pulled a beautiful big gold watch out of his pocket, and held it to the firelight to see what time it was.

"Where'd you get that?" I asked.

"I won it in a poker game," said Otis.

Joss grunted. "Who's carrying that kind of watch that you could win it playing poker?" he demanded.

"Well," said Otis, with a sly grin, "they say it originally belonged to a farmer up the road a piece."

"A farmer?" said Joss.

"He claimed to be a farmer," said Otis. "Some of our

boys figured he was one of these guerillas. Guerillas don't have any business having watches and things like that."

"So some of our boys inherited it, huh?" said Joss. "What'd the farmer have to say about it?"

"He didn't exactly have anything to say. You want to ask him, you can find him easy enough. He's just back up that road a little ways." He waved his hand off toward the south. "He's under a big tree."

"Under a tree, eh?" said Joss. "Are his feet touching the ground?"

"Well, no," drawled Otis. "Not unless somebody's cut him down real recently."

He went swaggering off, and I thought: Maybe that man really was a guerilla, in which case he ought to have been killed. But maybe he wasn't. If he wasn't, somebody has committed a murder, not to mention a robbery, and Otis is going around with that watch not seeing any harm in it. I remembered the kid he was the day he came to me down on the steamboat dock and said he was going to run off and join the army, and I shivered a little.

"Joss," I said grimly, "they better get this war over quick."

Joss shrugged.

"They better, but they won't," he said. "It's going to go on and on until the Rebs just can't fight any more. Right now they got quite a lot of fight left in 'em."

"But this Otis, now," I said. "He was always a nice kid. He wouldn't've been in on anything like that in the old days."

"You do a lot of things when you're a soldier you wouldn't've done in the old days," replied Joss. "Otis is one of Sheridan's scouts. They've got to be tough, those boys."

"But did they hang that man because they really thought he was a guerilla, or because he had a watch they wanted?"

Joss took off his forage cap and scratched his head.

"What difference does it make?" he asked. "When one of those guerillas kills one of our boys and takes his boots, does he kill him because he's fighting for his country or because he wants a new pair of boots? Anyway, one of these days the guerillas'll maybe catch Otis, and get that watch back."

That made me feel worse than ever, and I got up. I wanted to go find Otis and reason with him, although I didn't think it would do any good. More than that, I wanted to get off by myself for a while. It seemed to me that this war that Dr. Edwards had seen such high ideals in was turning mean and nasty, and I wanted to figure it out. But just then Shorty McNair, who was a headquarters orderly, came up.

"General wants to see you right away in his tent," he called to me.

Shorty, who was small, wore a skin-tight cavalry uniform with an extra-short jacket, and, from Heaven knew where, had lifted a pair of officer's riding boots, which he had shined so you could see your reflection in them. He kept his cap pulled down over his left eye, and was very cocky.

"Me?" I asked, stupidly.

"Why not? Better get moving. It don't do to keep the general waiting."

I knew that, but Shorty didn't have any business trying to hustle me, so I told him where he could go and what he could do to fill in his spare time along the way. Then I went over to the big tent fly that Sheridan had strung up in front of his sleeping tent.

The general was sitting on a canvas camp chair behind a plain kitchen table that had papers on it. Sitting beside him was Major Young, who had charge of all the scouts. Major Young was slim and clean-shaven, and looked older than he really was. When he smiled, which wasn't often, he had a way of just smiling with his mouth, so that his smiles never looked exactly friendly or jolly. His eyes were very hard. This evening he had on a Federal uniform.

Sheridan didn't waste any time coming to the point.

"That girl you know in Winchester," he said. "The doctor's daughter. She said she'd help us if we needed it."

"Yes, sir." I could feel a little twinge of excitement at his mention of Lavinia.

"I want you to take a letter to her and bring me back an answer," said Sheridan.

Again I said "Yes, sir," although I couldn't for the life of me see how I was going to get in and out of Winchester with the Rebel army all around the place. I'd told Lavinia and her father that General Sheridan would figure out a way, and I sure hoped he had figured out a good one.

The general took up a thin sheet of tissue paper, on which he had scribbled a few lines in pencil, and gave it to Major Young. The major folded it carefully, folded it again, creasing the fold hard, and kept on folding and refolding it until it was just a little flat wad no more than an inch long and a quarter-inch wide, with no thickness to speak of. Then he took a little square of tinfoil, put the note in it, and folded the tinfoil around it carefully. He creased the edges and pressed it flat, and Sheridan watched him. At last there was nothing to look at but that little silver-colored wafer.

Major Young looked up at me.

"You chew tobacco?" he said. Surprised, I told him, no, I didn't.

"Oh well——" The major handed the wafer to me.

"Hold this inside your mouth, between your upper lip and the gum," he directed. "Slide it along to the side if it makes your lip bulge out too much."

I took it and did as he said. He studied me critically.

"That'll do, I guess," he said. "If the Rebs catch you, swallow it the minute they lay hands on you, even if it chokes you—which it hadn't better. That little pellet is your death sentence, Sergeant, if the Rebs get hold of it."

He turned to Sheridan.

"Shall I give him a Reb outfit to wear, General?" he asked. Sheridan shook his head.

"Let him wear his own uniform. Then if he does get caught, and they don't find the letter, he has an outside chance of being held as a prisoner of war instead of as a spy."

Major Young smiled that cold little smile of his.

"An outside chance," he agreed. The two officers got up, and Sheridan turned to me.

"Go with Major Young," he said. "He'll get you into Winchester and tell you how to get out again. Give the girl the note and wait for an answer. Get it back here as soon as you can."

Then he stopped being the general, and punched me on the shoulder with one fist.

"Good luck to you, Sergeant," he said.

Major Young took me over to the cluster of tents where the scouts lived, and on the way explained what I was to do.

The scouts had recently found a free colored man who had a little farm on a byroad a few miles from camp. This man had a Confederate army pass allowing him to go in and out of Winchester with a wagon, peddling garden truck to the townspeople. Like every colored man I'd seen in the war, this man was all for the Union, and he'd agreed to smuggle me into Winchester and out again. He knew where the doctor's house was, so the plan was that he'd drive up an alley and drop me by the entrance to the doctor's carriage house. A couple of hours later he'd pick me up there, and with a lot of luck we'd go out through the Rebel lines and return to camp.

It sounded like a slim chance to me, and I asked the major if he was sure I ought to wear my uniform.

"It doesn't matter much," he said. "If the Rebs find you in the wagon they've got you, no matter what you're wearing. If anybody in Winchester sees you get in or out of the wagon, they've got you. You'll be reaching and leaving that house after dark, and your only chance is to avoid being seen at all. There's no moon, and it'll be good and dark tonight."

He looked at me in a curious way.

"You scared?" he asked.

"I just wanted to know," I said.

One of the scouts came up leading an extra horse, which

I mounted. Major Young wished me luck, in a voice that sounded as if he didn't really think I was going to have any, and the scout and I rode off. We got past our picket line all right, and just as the twilight was turning into night we came up to the free Negro's cabin.

It was a neat place, whitewashed, with a good-looking vegetable garden beside it, a field of sweet corn behind that, and a shed that did duty as a barn, in front of which was an ordinary farm wagon. A gray-headed colored man in shirt and pants that had been washed so many times there was no color left in them was loading the wagon with gunny sacks and baskets of produce.

"H'lo, Jeff," said the scout. "Here's the man we talked about. You gonna get him into Winchester tonight and then get him out again?"

The colored man looked at the scout, and then he looked at me. In the dark I couldn't see much of his face except for the whites of his eyes and his teeth. He nodded, and when he spoke he didn't have the mumble-jumble accent I thought all southern Negroes had.

"I'll get him in, and get him out again, too, if he does just what I tell him," he said.

"He will." The scout turned and reached for the reins of my horse. "He's Jeff Davis," he said, wagging his head toward the Negro. "Do what he says and you'll be all right. Good luck."

He rode off, leading the spare horse. I stood looking at this stranger who was going to hold my life in his hands, and wondered what I was to do.

As it turned out, it was quite simple. He had arranged his sacks and baskets so there was a space at the right side of the wagon box about a foot wide and nearly six feet long, where he made me lie down flat with a couple of empty sacks under me. Then he covered me with a pile of cornstalks, all green and leafy, and kept piling them on until the weight felt pretty heavy.

"Whatever happens, don't move until I tell you to," he said.

He went on loading the wagon, and soon I could hear him hitching a horse. Then he clucked to it and we went off down the road and headed for Winchester.

I believe if you could put a man's imagination to sleep, he'd never be afraid of anything. That trip was the simplest ride in the world, and there really wasn't any reason for me to be sweating so, down in the bottom of the wagon box. But I kept thinking of all the things that could go wrong. I listened for horses' hoofs, figuring a squad of guerillas would be riding up any minute; I could see them prying into Jeff's load, digging in under the cornstalks, hauling me out—and my mind kept making pictures of what they would do to me, once they caught me.

Yet nothing much actually happened. Once, some time after we'd started, I did hear a couple of horsemen ride up. They struck a light and looked at Jeff's pass, gave it back to him, and went away. At the regular Confederate picket post, on the edge of Winchester, the sentries looked at the pass again, and apparently they peeked into the wagon.

"Where you goin' with all that long forage, Uncle?" one of them said. When Jeff answered, he sounded like an ignorant plantation darky, slurring his words and talking very humble. He said something about Miz' Foster wanting some for her cow. One of the sentries spoke up.

"Miz' Foster? I know her," he said. "The Yankees burned her nephew's barn last week and carried off all his corn. She's been havin' a bad time."

He went on to explain, in a rambling way, how Miz' Foster was keeping a cow in a little stable back of her house here in Winchester, and how the army horses were eating up all the pasturage the animal usually had. He and the other sentry got into quite a talk about how much green stuff a cow ought to have, and how much grain, and what'd happen to the cow's milk if the proportions weren't right. At last they agreed it was a good thing Miz' Foster was getting these green cornstalks and leaves. Then the wagon wheels began to turn again and we went on into town.

In the town a patrol stopped us just once. Jeff showed his pass again and we moved on. After what seemed a long time, the wagon came to a stop and I could feel Jeff lifting the bundle of stalks off me. It was dark as pitch, and Jeff was whispering:

"Climb out now—easy; don't kick the sides of the wagon box. This is Dr. Edwards's carriage house."

I got down to the ground and stood there, trying to figure out which way was which. Jeff took me by the shoulders and turned me halfway around. I could just see the outlines of the dwelling house, twenty yards away.

"There's a light coming under the blind from the kitchen," he whispered. "Don't walk on the path when you go up there because the gravel will crunch. I'll be back for you at midnight."

A Night Ride to Winchester

I could hear the wagon squeak faintly as he climbed in, and it went trundling off in the dark. I stood there for a minute, everything dark and still. Then I walked up along the grass, waited by the back porch for a little to try to collect my wits. Then I reached up and tapped lightly on the kitchen door.

19. THE ONE THING I REMEMBERED

Nothing at all happened. Inside the house there was never a sound. It seemed as if I stood there for five minutes, rigid, hardly breathing, not moving for fear the porch floor boards would squeak. The town was quiet, and I could hear the trees rustling faintly in the night breeze. I had the notion that everybody was keeping quiet on purpose, just waiting for me to make a move and when I did, the whole town would come boiling out, yelling, carrying lights and pointing, while the patrols galloped up to get me.

After a while I began to get some sense. This porch ran along the back wing of the house for about a dozen feet, and a railing and some latticework were along the side on which wild cucumber vines grew, thick and solid. Where I was standing it was dark as dark could be; you couldn't have found a place where there was less risk of being seen by outsiders. As long as I didn't go out of my way to draw the neighbors' attention, I was safe enough.

I reached out to knock on the door again. This time I was going to pound hard. At the last minute, I changed my mind. Instead of knocking, I just opened the door, stepped inside, and shut the door behind me.

I was in an ordinary sort of kitchen, with a polished range opposite me and a long kitchen table beside it. On a stool at the table there was a colored woman with her hands in a big yellow bowl, kneading some sort of dough —yeast rolls for tomorrow morning's breakfast, as likely as not.

She stared at me without moving, considerably surprised to see a Union soldier there but not looking afraid or ready to yell or anything. She looked at me and I looked at her.

"Did you knock, just now?" she asked quietly.

I said I had.

"You ought to do it louder," she said. "I heard a tapping, but I thought it was the wind slapping the vines on the porch."

"I was afraid to make too much noise."

It seemed funny, us arguing about why I hadn't made more noise, as if that was any way important. Finally I got smart enough to ask her if Miss Lavinia was home.

"Who are you?" she asked.

"My name's Bob Hayden," I said. "I was here one night a couple of weeks ago. I told her I'd be coming back with a message for her."

The colored woman thought a minute, and her face lit up.

"Are the Lincoln soldiers back in town?" she asked eagerly.

I shook my head.

"Just me."

She got up and began to squeeze the dough off her fingers. As she did it she said they could hide me, all right, but she didn't see how I could ever get away, the patrols watched the streets so close. Then she gave her hands a final wipe on her apron and went away. In a minute I heard other footsteps, and Lavinia came in holding out her hand just as if it was perfectly natural for me to come calling when the town was full of Johnnies. I thought once more what a firm, strong, sort of honest little hand she had.

"I brought you a letter, ma'am," I said.

She watched while I got that little tinfoil packet out of my mouth. While I was unfolding it she said: "Your lip did look swollen. I thought maybe you'd been in a fight." I got the tissue paper out of the tinfoil and handed it to her, and she moved nearer to the lamp and unfolded it. I watched her as she read, frowning a little, trying to make out the smudgy penciled script on the thin paper in the lamplight. When she finished she turned to me and smiled.

"After he signs his name," she said, "General Sheridan says: 'You can trust the bearer.' Can I?"

I said, "Yes, ma'am," feeling sort of foolish.

"He wants to know things I don't really know myself," she said, after a moment. She studied the letter again and read aloud: ". . . the position of Early's forces, the number of divisions in his army, the strength of any or all of them . . . his reported intentions."

I thought I could help her a little.

"What he wants to know most of all is whether Early has

sent any of his troops back to Richmond. I think so, any-how. That's what they're saying around headquarters."

She looked more hopeful.

"I do know something about that." She hesitated, and then said: "Let's go in and talk with Father."

She led me into the living room. Dr. Edwards was there in his rocker, an open book in his lap. He held out a hand to me as if he was not at all surprised to see me, and asked what sort of trip I'd had: you'd have thought I'd just come in by train. I told him the trip had been all right, and Lavinia gave him Sheridan's letter. After he had read it she told him what I had said.

"Couldn't I tell him about Kershaw's division?" she asked. The doctor nodded. She went to a little desk to get a sheet of writing paper, but I suggested:

"Why don't you write it on the back of General Sheri-dan's letter? Then we can fold it up small and put it in the tinfoil like it was before."

She nodded, and to her father she said: "Bob brought this letter here in his mouth. Under his upper lip." Then, as she picked up a pencil and laid the paper face down so that she could write on it, she looked at me, smiled, and said: "You forgot to say 'ma'am.'" So I said it and we both laughed. She tapped her teeth with the end of the pencil, then bent over the desk and wrote a few lines.

"I know General Kershaw's division has gone back to Richmond," she said, looking up at me. "So has Cutshaw's artillery—twelve guns. The whole of it is in General Ander-son's command. People say they aren't coming back. I don't know how many men General Early has, but I do know his army is much smaller than it's supposed to be. I wrote all of that to your general."

"Don't sign the letter," I said, as a sudden thought struck me.

"If the Rebs catch me and get hold of it, there's no sense letting them hang both of us."

She sobered at once, and the dancing light died out of her eyes. I felt angry with myself for saying "hang." Still, both she and the doctor were running a big risk, and there wasn't any sense in trying to make out they weren't. Yet I really believe that what had sobered her was not the thought of her own danger, but just the mental picture of a Confederate patrol seizing me and hauling me off as a spy.

The doctor asked how I intended to get back. I explained about Jeff, and said he would be around to pick me up before long. I told how the patrols and sentries had stopped us on the way in without bothering to see what was under the wagonload and the doctor gave a dry, mirthless, little chuckle.

"It will be pretty late at night, on the return trip," he said. "Let's hope they are all very sleepy."

We folded the letter as carefully as we could, got it back into the tinfoil, and managed to make a packet about like the original. It would be at least an hour before Jeff would come by, and the doctor suggested I ought to have something to eat. Soon I was sitting at the living-room table, eating a big slab of apple pie and drinking a glass of milk while the doctor and I talked. Lavinia didn't have much to say. She just sat there and looked at me, with worry in her gray eyes.

The One Thing I Remembered

At last it was time for me to go out and wait for Jeff there in the deepest shadow by the corner of the carriage house, so the doctor shook hands and wished me luck. I tucked the tinfoil packet under my upper lip, and Lavinia led me to the kitchen. The colored woman had finished with her dough and gone off to bed, and the kitchen lamp had been put out. The doctor told us not to relight it, so that no light would shine out when we opened the door.

The kitchen was nearly dark, with only a little light coming in from the hall doorway. I walked over to the back door, and as I reached for the knob Lavinia stood with her shoulder against the door.

"Please do be careful," she whispered.

It struck me that for the next few hours there wasn't much I could do along that line—everything would be up to Jeff, and up to luck—but I didn't say so. Instead I promised that I would, and that I'd come back soon. She didn't say anything, and in the dimness I could not see the expression on her face.

"I'll say goodbye now, because once the door is open we mustn't make a sound," I told her.

"Of course." She moved away from the door and I opened it, very quietly, and stepped out on the porch. In the darkness I felt her hand on my sleeve; she pulled me toward her, and suddenly her lips touched my mouth. I had never dreamed anything could feel so soft and gentle. Then I heard a faint little whisper: "Goodbye, Bob!" and as I reached for her she stepped back. The door was softly closed and latched as she went back into the house. I was alone in the darkness.

Somehow I got down the steps and walked back to the

corner. I even remembered Jeff's warning, and walked on
the lawn so as not to make a noise on the gravel. The night
was one big shadow, thinned out just a little overhead.
Maybe there were a few stars: I don't know for sure, because even though there were thousands of Rebel soldiers
between me and safety, all I could think of just then was
Lavinia and the way her mouth had touched mine.

I don't know how long I stood there but at last I heard
a faint noise down the lane, and along came Jeff in his
wagon. He pulled up and reached into the shadow and
touched my shoulder. I believe Jeff could see in the dark
like a cat.

Very carefully I climbed into the wagon. The cornstalks
and garden truck were all gone, and the wagon was half
full of empty baskets and limp gunny sacks. Jeff had me
lie down, and strewed the sacks and old baskets over me.
In daylight, I suppose, anyone could have seen that there
was somebody under all that stuff, but in the dark or in
the half light of a campfire it might be all right. When he
had things the way he wanted them we went trundling
off.

I had expected to be tense and nervous, but I wasn't.
Patrols and sentries stopped us a few times, looked at Jeff's
pass, took a casual glance into the littered wagon, and
waved us on. We never moved faster than a walk, and
whenever Jeff had to say anything he sounded like a sleepy
back-country darky with nothing on his mind except the
idea of getting home and going to bed.

As I lay there under the sacking, half conscious of that
wedge of tinfoil under my lip, I wasn't thinking about the
dust or the bumpy ride or the things the Rebel patrols

would do if they caught on to the kind of load Jeff was hauling. On the earlier trip I'd been worried all the time, but on this one I wasn't worried at all. All I could think of was that one moment on the dark porch when Lavinia kissed me.

20. THE GENERAL PAYS A CALL

The road that crosses Opequon Creek leads up to Winchester through a shallow valley with steep wooded banks. The valley is so narrow and the road so winding there is room for only one file of wagons or one column of marching men. When Sheridan's army came up the road, in the cool early morning of September 19, we got into a tangle that almost cost us a battle.

Lavinia's letter had told Sheridan exactly what he wanted to know. Early had sent troops away: so Sheridan moved promptly.

We came up from Harpers Ferry on the main road, then sideslipped south of the creek, crossing the water before dawn and coming up toward Winchester from the east. The infantry would make its fight as soon as we got out of this valley. Meanwhile, a division of cavalry would swing to the left to cut in behind the Rebs, while two other cavalry divisions came down from the north and hit the Rebs on the other flank; taking one thing with another, Sheridan figured he would destroy Early's whole army before sunset.

But it didn't work that way. We crossed the creek all right, the cavalry scattering the Johnnies' patrols, and the tough old Sixth Corps went marching up the valley, ready for a fight—and then everything went wrong.

Orders got mixed up—which seldom happened, under Sheridan—and a whole wagon train got wedged in back of the Sixth Corps, blocking the way for the rest of the army. Because the road and the valley were so narrow, the wagon train couldn't turn around and go back and it couldn't just pull off the road to let the infantry and the guns get by. It just had to keep going, a jolting, clumsy, lumbering procession not moving two miles an hour, and everybody else had to follow it. There wasn't anything even Sheridan could do to set things straight.

When the Sixth Corps boys got to the Reb position and began to fight, there wasn't anybody to help them and for several hours they had to fight alone. Sheridan had figured that he would come in on Early with enough men to mash him, while his cavalry would crumple the Rebel flanks. Instead, when the fight started there were more Rebs than Union men present, and all morning we had a mean, wearing fight in which it often looked as if we were in for a bad licking.

I've never had so much hard riding to do. Sheridan was driving big Rienzi so hard the animal's black coat was all streaked with foam, and since Sheridan always wanted his flag with him, I had to gallop at his heels wherever he went. I was glad then that I didn't weigh very much for if Red had had any more to carry he'd have given out, sure. Whenever we'd pull to a halt, even a short one, I'd jump off and try to give him a little rest.

Along the battle line the musketry fire was unbroken. The Rebs had a lot of artillery up on high ground that hammered away as fast as the guns could be handled. A lot of our boys were hurt, and the battle made a wild, insane noise that beat on your eardrums and made you think you'd give anything for just one minute of quiet. The air was full of dust and smoke like a fog, putting a flat metallic taste on your tongue and a dryness at the back of your throat. The air was laced and humming with the ugly whine of ricocheted bullets and flying pieces of shell.

For once Sheridan wasn't spending all his time on the firing line. He was hurrying around trying to clear the roads, to get more infantry forward, to see that the guns were brought up, to hurry the ammunition wagons.

When part of our battle line broke and the Rebs came swarming in over a little hill, jeering as if they were going to run us all the way back into Maryland, Sheridan led a fresh brigade in a counterattack, and stayed with it until he was sure nothing more would come loose. But the rest of the time he was storming around back of the lines, straightening out the kinks that kept him from putting all his men in line.

It was late afternoon before he had things fixed the way he wanted them. I was all confused, myself. As far as I could see, the battle had been a wild free-for-all ever since sunrise, and nine hours later it didn't look a bit better. Then, all of a sudden, the scattered pieces began to slip into place, and before I knew it we were winning.

Sheridan had been putting a number of guns on a knoll, near the right of his line. When they opened fire he went full speed to the left, and pulled up in a cloud of dust beside some general there and had a shouted conversation. Then he headed back to the right again, while our infantry began to advance all along the line, steady as if it was on parade. As the men began to go forward, along came Sheridan, waving his hat, his uniform dark with sweat, his flag bobbing along just behind him—riding at a full gallop the length of the battle line between our boys and the Johnnies.

Sheridan was pointing toward the Rebel line, shouting something I couldn't make out, and our boys were cheering—and me, I was holding onto the flagstaff, blindly hoping the Lord would let me live another sixty seconds, which didn't seem likely. On the higher ground the artillery was crashing and banging . . . all at once I realized that we were going to win, that Sheridan had things fixed at last, and that all of Early's soldiers couldn't stop us. I heard myself yelling along with the rest.

We pulled up on a hilltop. One of Sheridan's staff officers rode up, shouting and pointing to the west. I looked where he was pointing and what I saw I'll remember as long as I live.

In front of us, in a line two miles wide, was the Union infantry, swinging ahead with regimental flags waving, the lines as regular as if someone had painted a picture for a book. Beyond, several miles off, I could see the open fields bordering the road that goes into Winchester from the north; and along these fields were two divisions of Yankee cavalry, charging at a gallop, drawn sabers glinting in the afternoon sun, breaking in the flank of the Confederate battle line.

Away back at Grand Rapids, Joss Pettit had said that

troopers hardly ever used their sabers and the noble cavalry charges we read about were mostly just stories told for stay-at-homes—and so far in the war I had seen that he knew what he was talking about. But here for once it was like what I used to imagine it must be like before I knew better—five thousand troopers riding in a headlong charge, capturing Rebel batteries and overrunning an infantry firing line—and then the whole battle came apart. In the smoky twilight the field was full of cheering men tossing their caps. As the firing died down, Sheridan rode forward through the sunset glow, and the tired infantry pointed at him and yelled to one another: "There's Phil! There he is! There's Phil!" Jubilant officers came up to report, and Sheridan kept telling them to pull their troops together and keep going—the Johnnies were in full retreat, and he wanted to get in behind them, cut them off, and capture their whole army.

It turned out that could not be done. The Rebs went away fast, streaming south on the Valley Pike out of Winchester, but we couldn't quite get ahead of them for all of Sheridan's driving, and we had to be content with the victory that had been won.

It looked like a big victory to me. All of the mistakes that had cost so much early in the day had at last been overcome. If the Confederate army had not been destroyed, at least it had been badly beaten. Our cavalry rode through the town, sweeping up stragglers and walking wounded, and went on south to keep the beaten army moving. Infantry regiments collected themselves, long files of prisoners were plodding back to the rear, some of Sheridan's scouts were hallooing and cavorting around a park of captured cannon, and a long string of ambulances was creaking off to the field hospitals with hundreds of wounded men. The victory hadn't come cheap. Where the fighting lines had been, the burial details were digging long pits to take the bodies of men whose fighting was over forever.

Somewhere in Winchester, Sheridan pulled up to establish temporary headquarters on the open porch of a house, and he sat on the steps, his tousled hair all matted with sweat, while officers came up to report. I got Red's bridle off and haltered him under a tree in the back yard, where the other headquarters horses were picketed. With some of the other boys I got a fire going and boiled some coffee and ate a little hardtack. Then we lounged on the grass in the dusk, wishing we could call it a day and turn in but knowing perfectly well that Sheridan would find plenty for all of us to do before headquarters closed up shop for the night.

Sure enough: in a minute that dapper little orderly, Shorty McNair, came around the house in his skin-tight uniform. He stood in front of me and grinned.

"Get your horse and go round in front—the general wants you," he said.

I got up. I was stiff all over, caked with dried sweat and dust and streaked with smoke, and I thought I'd give anything on earth to be able to stretch out and stay stretched out for a week, and twice that much to be halfway clean again. I went over to Red wearily, took off his halter, put on his bridle, and led him around the corner of the house.

Sheridan was sitting at the top of the steps talking to

a couple of generals. His dark face glowing with enthusiasm, he was telling these generals something, hammering a palm with his fist for emphasis, and they were looking up at him as if they thought he was the greatest man they'd ever seen—which, I believe, is exactly what they did think.

He saw me while I was twenty feet away, broke off, and got to his feet.

"Excuse me, gentlemen," he said. "I've a little errand I must do now." He picked up his hat, gave the two generals some final word or other, called out something to his chief of staff, who was working with some papers at a camp table on the porch, and came stumping over to where I was waiting. An orderly brought up a horse—not Rienzi: he'd had too much of a workout that day.

"Now, Sergeant," said Sheridan to me, "I want you to take me to the house of the young lady who wrote me that letter."

I certainly didn't want Lavinia to see me until I had a chance to get cleaned up, because right then I wasn't a fit object to get near a young lady. Neither was Sheridan, for the matter of that. But a sergeant doesn't argue with a major general, so I said "Yes, sir," while we both mounted, and I rode down the street with General Sheridan at my side.

In a minute or two we were in that shady side street, and were turning in at the gate, dismounting, and tethering our horses. As we walked up to the house I could see Lavinia and Dr. Edwards sitting on the front porch, and just as I saw them Lavinia recognized me. The doctor got to his feet as she came down the steps and ran across the lawn, crying: "Bob!"

The next thing I knew she had her arms around my neck and was hugging me, and I seemed to have my arms around her. I was happy and unhappy, proud and embarrassed, wondering what the general was making of all of this, wishing that I was cleaned up, dizzy because she wanted to hug me—then I got hold of her wrists and pulled her arms away and said:

"Lavinia! I'm too dirty to touch! I'm awful dirty!"

She was laughing and repeating: "Bob! You're safe! You're safe!"

Then I heard Sheridan chuckling, and saying:

"Won't you introduce me to this young lady?"

Lavinia hadn't noticed him before, and it took her by surprise; when she saw the straps on his shoulders, and then heard me say that this was General Sheridan, her eyes got big and she stopped laughing. She didn't flutter, though, coming down to earth, the way a lot of girls would have done. She just put out her hand, and when Sheridan took it and made a little bow over it, she stood there, all five slim feet of her, as if she'd been used to meeting major generals all of her life.

Sheridan thanked her for sending him the letter, and told her that because of it we had won a victory that would help to settle how the war was going to come out, and said that he and the army and the whole country were indebted to her. Dr. Edwards came limping over, and Sheridan shook his hand and told him that he had a fine daughter. Then he and I were back at the gate, getting ready to mount and ride back to headquarters.

"I'd detail the sergeant to spend the evening here, but we have to keep moving," Sheridan called to Lavinia, as he swung into the saddle. "Some day soon, though, I'll send him back here." He grinned at me, and added: "After he's had a chance to clean up."

We rode off. There was a thin reek of powder smoke in the air, darkness had come, and we could hear, not far off, all of the two dozen different kinds of noise an army can make after a battle. I looked back at Lavinia standing by the gateway, and as we went round the corner she waved.

21. THE FARAWAY GUNS

Phil Sheridan kept his word, although nearly a month passed before he was able to.

It was a busy month. We marched up the Shenandoah Valley, with Early's tattered army fading back before us, and there was headquarters gossip that we would go all the way—turn east at the upper end of the Valley and come down on Richmond along the line of the James River. Grant wanted it done that way, figuring that with the help of Sheridan's army he could make Lee surrender before winter came.

But Sheridan was against it. For one thing, he knew there was still a lot of fight left in Early's army. It had been licked but it hadn't been knocked out, and until it was, Sheridan thought he would be taking a long chance to march east, leaving Early in his rear. Besides, the Valley was still full of guerillas, and Sheridan hated the idea of letting them swarm all over his line of supply.

So finally, in the middle of October, we turned around, came back down the Valley, and camped on a chain of low hills behind Cedar Creek, about twenty miles south of

Winchester. The Johnnies followed us, and when we camped they camped, too, five miles south of us. We lolled around the headquarters tents, enjoying the fine autumn weather and wondering what was going to happen next.

Then General Sheridan decided to make a quick trip to Washington to find out how the War Department wanted the rest of the fall campaign handled.

With several staff officers, Sheridan rode over to Front Royal to take the cars to Washington. He left word that he would come back by way of Martinsburg, and ordered a cavalry escort sent to Winchester to meet him. And just before he went he called me into his tent. He gave me a very hard look.

"Sergeant," he said, "I'm going to Washington for a day or so. While I'm gone, I detail you to look after Dr. Edwards. And his daughter, of course."

He scowled. From his air, he might have been sending me to the guardhouse.

"You stay in Winchester and see that no harm comes to these people. When my escort meets me and I go back to camp, you come along. Until then——"

He broke off, and winked.

"That town is Sesesch," he said. "We've got to look out for our friends."

In occupied towns, many times, guards would be detailed to protect certain families. Sometimes they were there to protect them against our own stragglers and marauders, who had developed pretty rowdy habits in four years of war, and sometimes they were supposed to keep Reb sympathizers from getting rough with people who had been friendly to us. But Dr. Edwards and Lavinia didn't really need any protection, and Sheridan knew that I knew it. He was just giving me a little holiday pretending it was business.

That was how it was I spent two days at the Edwards house.

In a way it was like being home and having the war over. I slept in a good bed with clean white sheets, ate home-cooked food at a dining table with a white cloth on it, and had somebody besides soldiers to look at and listen to. Evenings, Lavinia and I would walk under the big trees, with the dry autumn leaves rustling under our feet, while we talked about all sorts of things. Later, the three of us would sit in the living room and Dr. Edwards would ask me questions about Michigan, and about what I intended to do after the war was over, while Lavinia brought a pitcher of milk and slices of cake in from the kitchen.

Until then I had never thought much about what I would do after the war. It seemed as if I had always been in the army and always would be. I never tried to plan for the future, because in the army somebody else always does the planning for you. But now we were on the downhill stretch. For the first time since I'd enlisted it seemed reasonable to look ahead and think about what was going to happen afterward.

I'd been taking it for granted that if the war ever did end, I would just go back to what I'd been doing before, without any particular change. Now I began to understand that I would be beginning something new instead of going back to something old. I might go back to the place where I had always lived—as a matter of fact, I wanted to—but I would be a different person. I had changed even if the place itself hadn't changed, and the war itself had been so big that nothing was ever going to be quite the way it was in the old days.

I tried to say all of that, the last evening I was in the Edwards house; but all at once it seemed that I had been talking too much, and I got confused and stopped, feeling guilty. Lavinia kept looking at me without saying anything. Dr. Edwards smiled, in a friendly way, and asked:

"You're not afraid to go back, are you?"

"Afraid?"

I'd never thought of it that way. "Why, no, sir, of course not. What is there to be afraid of?"

"Change," he said, quietly. "Most people fear change more than they fear anything else on earth. We're rather like cats, you know. We want everything to be the same as it always has been. We hate to get out of the familiar groove. It may not be a very good groove but we're used to it, and if we get out of it we'll have to make new decisions and steer new courses. That doesn't frighten you?"

I shook my head. It would have frightened me, once: but how could one of Phil Sheridan's best troopers be afraid of making his own way in the world?

The doctor went on:

"We'll probably have some difficult years, once the war is over. We blundered into this war because we were afraid of change, and we thought if we fought hard enough we could keep change from happening. Now we're going to find that everything has changed, that the change will go on and on for as long as any of us are alive, and it will be hard to adjust to that fact."

He smiled at me.

"Just don't be afraid of it and you'll be all right," he said.

I felt like saying that if Lavinia would go with me I would never be afraid of anything, but I couldn't quite find the words. While I was groping for them, she spoke up.

"You're going back to camp in the morning, aren't you, Bob?"

She knew perfectly well I was. Sheridan's cavalry escort was camped in a field just south of town, and I was to join it at dawn. Sheridan would be along about six o'clock, and we'd take him back to the army lines at Cedar Creek.

"I'm worried," she said, unexpectedly. "I'm afraid something terrible is going to happen."

This didn't sound like her, and I wondered what was coming.

"You know," she went on, "the people in this town have funny ways of learning things. The Confederate army is twenty-five miles away, and our army"—it always made me feel good, inside, to hear her say *our* army—"our army is camped between. Yet somehow the people here keep in touch. They have ways of knowing what is going on."

There was a shadow in her eyes as she looked from me to her father and then back to me.

"They're expecting something," she said. "I don't know just what it is, but I can tell from the way they look and from little remarks they've let fall. Early is going to do something big. The townspeople know just enough about it to be all excited. They think our army is going to get whipped."

"Well," I tried to reassure her, "General Sheridan will be

back first thing in the morning. Nothing bad can happen as long as he's around."

She shook her head.

"I wish he hadn't gone away at all," she said. "This may happen before he gets back here."

Somehow I couldn't worry very much. Sheridan would be back in the morning, nothing could go wrong if he was there, and there was hardly time, now, for anything much to happen before he got back. I put it all out of my mind, and settled down to make the most of this last evening.

I was busy, anyhow, thinking about what was going to happen after the war. I knew I was going back home, that there was a place for me in Uncle Ebenezer's business; indeed, I knew that some day, if I worked hard and showed good sense, it would be my business, and because that whole part of the state was growing and developing there would be a good chance to do very well with it. In one way I didn't have much to worry about.

Yet I was discovering now that when I began to think about my own future Lavinia seemed to be all mixed up in it. If she could be there, too, then I wanted to go back to that little town, work hard, and make a home of my own; and if she wasn't ever going to be there, then I didn't want to go back there myself. I wanted to tell her so, yet I couldn't seem to figure out just how to say it. I suppose down under everything I was afraid of what she might say if I did tell her, so I didn't say anything.

I got up before dawn next morning, and she gave me breakfast. We were silent while I ate and she sat at the table and watched me. I finished, got my things together, and went out to the carriage house, saddled Red and made ready to leave. When at last I was standing there, with the reins in my fist, she was standing on the grass by the end of the gravel walk, looking at me, with worry in her eyes. I didn't know whether she was worried about me, or about the army, or about things in general, and I tried to tell her that everything was going to be all right, but I guess I didn't do it very well.

At last I said: "Well, I guess I'd better go."

She moved a little closer. "Bob, please do be careful," and everything she was worried about seemed to be in her voice.

"I'll be all right. I'll come back, for sure."

I wanted to put my arms around her and tell her lots of things, but like a miserable fool I had the notion that it might spoil everything I was hoping for because that might not be what she wanted me to do at all, so I just stood there and gaped at her, like a schoolboy. I swung up into the saddle, finally, and said again: "I'll come back."

I turned quickly, Red trotted down the alley, and she was out of sight.

It was a cool, clear October morning, and as I rode out toward the field where the escort was bivouacked, the town and the countryside were quiet. Then, away off toward the south, I heard a faint noise like distant rumbling thunder. I listened without thinking much about it; then I realized that it didn't sound like thunder at all. Somewhere, off where the army was, the artillery was firing.

I rode faster, and got to the field just as the boys were finishing breakfast. I sat on a little knoll, Red nibbled at the grass while the cavalry saddled up, and all the time, down beyond the horizon, there was that noise—a mild, fluttering sort of sound, with faint bumps and quivers in it, that sounded harmless until you realized what was making it.

It didn't sound like heavy firing, as if a big battle was going on, but it was pretty steady just the same: and I couldn't help remembering that Lavinia had been worried. Now and then I could see one or another of the officers cock his head to listen, but nobody seemed to be especially bothered and I figured they probably knew more about what was going on than I did.

Pretty soon Sheridan and two or three of his staff came jingling up. Sheridan dismounted and listened, and asked somebody how long the firing had been going on. I heard one of the cavalry officers tell him that General Wright, who was in charge of the army in Sheridan's absence, had planned to tap the Reb lines this morning just to see how strong they were, and Sheridan nodded as if that was enough to account for the racket.

But as we mounted and started off for Cedar Creek, and I fell into line right behind the general with the flagstaff in my hand, I noticed that he was frowning a little, and once in a while he would rein in to listen.

We kept on going, and the noise grew just a bit louder. Once Sheridan called a halt, waved his hand for us to keep quiet, and got off his horse, bending over to get his ear nearer to the ground so that he could hear better. When he straightened up he remarked, to nobody in particular: "That's getting closer." When he remounted he set a faster pace, and the whole cavalcade moved at a good sharp trot.

You couldn't have asked for a prettier morning. Off to

the right and left the open country rolled away to the mountains. Everything was autumn colors—scarlet, gold, and brown—with a thin blue haze over it all. Things couldn't have been more peaceful . . . except that the bump-flutter of the firing was always there, a little louder now, and a good deal more distinct, so that you could tell the brassy clang of the twelve-pounder smoothbores from the crisp report of the three-inch rifles.

After climbing a long easy slope, we got to the crest and looked down the Valley Pike, stretching out for miles ahead of us. It was like watching the bottom fall out of everything.

★

22. *AND THE SIXTH CORPS CHEERED*

Coming toward us was a wild, leaderless, mixed-up crowd of beaten men and animals—a wagon train clattering along with teamsters flogging exhausted horses; artillery caissons, battery forges, and forage wagons, strings of led horses, headquarters outfits, kitchen details, and ambulances, some loaded and some empty. In and around and all about, spreading out over the fields for half a mile on each side of the turnpike, were disorganized infantrymen.

Whatever Lavinia had been afraid of had happened. Sheridan's army had been driven in a wild, disorganized rout.

Some of the infantry in the fields were grouped about little campfires, boiling coffee. Most of them were slouching along as if they didn't mean to stop this side of the Potomac. I noticed that they were carrying their guns and didn't seem to be in any great hurry. Now and then one or two would pull up, turn, and listen to the distant firing. But I had seen enough battles to know that they were acting exactly the way routed soldiers always act, once they've got back out of cannon range.

Routed men don't run at top speed, except maybe for a few rods right at first. They just saunter along, as if the fighting were no concern of theirs. They don't even act scared. They keep ambling along, and although they move slowly they are exactly like a runaway team of horses— it's almost impossible to stop them until they themselves decide that they have gone far enough.

Sheridan pulled up abruptly and looked at all of this, his swarthy face growing black. He snapped a word to one of his staff officers and the man went rocketing ahead as fast as his horse would take him. The rest of us sat there and stared with our mouths open. We just couldn't believe what we were seeing.

In a minute the staff man came back at a gallop. I heard him tell Sheridan that the Johnnies had attacked before daylight and had taken our army completely by surprise. The whole of the Eighth Corps and a good part of the Nineteenth Corps had gone all to pieces. The Rebs had our camps, a lot of our cannon, and hundreds of prisoners. General Wright was supposed to be forming some sort of battle line four or five miles this side of Cedar Creek, which was probably where the banging was coming from now, but the people the staff man had talked with didn't think General Wright's line would hold. As far as they were concerned, our army was licked and licked for keeps.

I expected Sheridan to storm and swear, but I might have known better; it was when everybody else was all excited and nervous that he was most likely to be calm and quiet. He leaned forward in his saddle, now, and rapped out his orders fast, but he didn't raise his voice. He didn't have time to waste cussing.

Most of the cavalry escort and some of his staff officers were sent down the road to stop the retreat, get the wagons off the road and into the fields, and make the infantry fall into ranks. Nobody was to be allowed to get one foot closer to Winchester than the hilltop where we then were.

Then with two or three officers, a handful of cavalry, and me carrying the flag, Sheridan started down the road for Cedar Creek, riding as fast as Rienzi would take him.

We went past the first of the wagons and caissons, where our troopers were swearing and jerking at bridles to get the teams headed off the road, making a cloud of dust heavy as a fog. When we came out into the open road again and got abreast of the first knot of walking infantry, Sheridan snatched off his hat, crumpled it in his fist, and swung it in the sweeping gesture I had seen so many times.

"Turn back, men—turn back!" he shouted. "This army isn't beaten! We'll lick 'em yet! Turn back!"

The men gaped at him, unbelieving. Then they recognized him, and suddenly they began to toss their hats into the air and yell. Some of them actually jumped up and down with excitement. I saw men calling to comrades farther off in the field, pointing to Sheridan and calling: "Look! There's Phil! There's Phil!"

Then we were past, going on at a full gallop: and to every man or group within earshot, Sheridan was calling, over and over: "Turn around, boys—turn around! We're going to get our camps back!"

Once we saw a number of wounded men sprawled under a clump of trees, with surgeons working over them. Sheridan dismounted and walked over to them. Although he was moving pretty fast, he made you feel he was perfectly calm and unhurried and had all the time in the world; and when you watched him it was impossible to believe that anything very serious could have gone wrong.

"Boys, this wouldn't have happened if I'd been here," he told the wounded men. "It's going to be all right. You'll see. We'll get our camps back."

The wounded men nodded their heads and believed him. Men who had been standing around the edges heard him and turned to call and wave to other men who were standing farther away; then Sheridan was on Rienzi again and we were off, going at a full gallop, raising a wind that snapped and flapped the little two-starred flag so that I could feel the staff vibrate.

Once or twice we pulled up, while Sheridan said a few words to men close by the road. He spoke quietly, cool as a cucumber—not angry at anybody for running away or worried for fear that it might be too late to turn defeat into victory; just relaxed and easy, as if there wasn't a doubt in the world but that everybody would turn around, go back to the battle line, and regain everything that had been lost.

One time he had me go to a little clump of scrub trees and cut a switch for him, so that he could get a little more speed out of Rienzi. But for the most part we kept going without stopping, and as we rode Sheridan kept swinging his hat and calling out:

"Turn back, men! Turn back!"

The response was always the same—something I

wouldn't have believed unless I had seen it myself, because I knew from experience how next to impossible it is to make routed men turn around and head back into battle.

The men would stare, then wave their hats and yell, call to the men farther out in the fields, point to the general, and shout: "Sheridan! Sheridan! Sheridan!"

Some of the men fired their muskets in the air, to draw the attention of those who were too far away to hear what they were saying. I could see those men, half a mile off, pull up and look—then they would wave their arms and start to move in toward the road. Groups of men sitting around campfires would jump up, kick over their coffeepots, and grab their stacked muskets. All the way along the Valley Pike we were followed by a steady, rising wave of sound—cheers and laughter and gay shouts, with a thickening column of men under it; and we could hear men yelling: "Sheridan! Sheridan!" as if they were chanting a name that held a mighty magic.

And it did have magic. Ahead of us, the fields were blue with crowds of aimless stragglers. As we passed, it was as if someone had tilted the whole landscape so that the fields all drained into the road, and behind us we could see a lengthening blue column taking form on the dusty white turnpike.

Most of the men were too far away to hear what Sheridan was saying, but that didn't seem to matter. They saw him, the stocky figure on the big black horse, saw his great gestures and his hard bullet head, saw his two-starred flag snapping in the wind, saw their comrades waving their hats, pointing and crying: "There's Phil!"—

and the magic caught them. In a twinkling they turned from runaways into good soldiers again.

We kept going a long time, through the little village of Middletown; then ahead of us, stretched out to the right of the road, we saw General Wright's line of battle. Field artillery was on the high ground, banging away now and then with the Rebel guns firing back, but it was all long-range stuff and nobody seemed to be taking it very seriously. Clearly there was a lull in the battle, for the moment.

When Sheridan saw the men who had not run away, all drawn up in line ready to go on with the fighting whenever anyone said the word, his face grew dark again. Looking at those who hadn't panicked seemed to make him furious at the ones who had, and his manner changed. We came up through a lot of floaters—lost infantrymen, artillerists who had got separated from their guns, cavalrymen who had lost their horses—and Sheridan jammed his hat on his head and whipped out his saber.

"Turn around, you cowardly curs!" he shouted. The edge on his voice was sharp enough to cut your throat. "Turn around or I'll cut you down. I know you don't like to fight, but"—he swung his arm pointing that saber at the battle line ahead, and the sunlight gleamed on the metal as if he were swinging a flaming sword—"come on up and look at men who *do!*"

The battle line was mostly made up of the Sixth Corps, those case-hardened veterans from the Army of the Potomac. They were lounging in the ranks, and they confessed afterward that they had been puzzled by the sound of cheering off to the rear. Behind them, they knew, was nothing but the raveled fringes of the army—the walking wounded, the demoralized, the scared fugitives . . . and what on earth, the veterans were asking themselves, could *those* characters have to cheer about?

While the veterans were puzzling over this, there came a drumming of hoofs, and a little cavalcade swept down the road, swerved sharply, and galloped straight along the battle line, a dozen paces in front—and the man at the head of the group was the only one anybody saw because that man was Sheridan, swinging his hat and calling out his greeting to the soldiers who had not run away.

These Sixth Corps boys had learned to like Sheridan, but they were old-timers who had been through the mill and it was a matter of pride with them not to cheer any generals no matter what happened. But this morning, as Sheridan rode down the line, the veterans stared at him for a few seconds, and all at once the whole army corps blew up with the wildest cheer I ever heard in all my life.

Men sounded hysterical with joy. They threw hats, canteens, and haversacks into the air, jumped up and down, slapped each other on the back, yelled until their voices broke. Rienzi seemed to think the cheers were for him, and pranced and bowed as he went along the line. Sheridan kept calling out to the soldiers, but they were making such a steady uproar nobody could hear what he was saying, and it didn't matter because everybody knew that we would go on and win the battle now that Sheridan was back.

And that's exactly what we did, although it was well on in the afternoon before the battle was resumed. It took time to get the returning stragglers organized and put into line—and what an unmerciful roasting the veterans gave those men, as they stumbled sheepishly into their places. Sheridan wasn't going to move until he had everything ready, but at last he gave the word, and the whole line went forward. Soon Sheridan himself was lancing back and forth across the front, pulling the men on—and at last the whole Rebel line broke. As dusk came down, our boys were sweeping back over the camps they had lost, and the Rebs were in wild retreat.

The sun had gone down, the fight was over, and Early's army was wrecked for keeps. All of the guns we had lost were recaptured, along with a lot of Rebel guns. We had our old camps back, just as Sheridan had promised, and far to the south our cavalry was rocketing around, capturing wagons and stragglers and turning retreat into rout.

Sheridan stood in front of his headquarters tents, looking proudly into the firelit clearing. Those harum-scarum scouts of his, togged out in Confederate uniforms and brandishing captured Confederate battle flags, were riding around the campfire, yelling and capering like so many red Indians.

Sheridan stood by a rank of captured cannon, leaning against one of the guns and quietly, absent-mindedly patting the satiny metal with one hand.

The war in the Shenandoah Valley had been won; without the Valley, Lee's army could not hope to hold Richmond much longer, and the dancing firelight in the clearing was an omen of the final sunset for the Confederacy.

Sheridan knew it, and he stood there with the red light of the flames glinting off his swarthy cheekbones, his eyes aglow. The shadows of the prancing riders leaped and danced grotesquely against the tents, but I don't think Sheridan saw them. He was looking beyond them, seeing the end of the war.

23. IT'S JUST BEGINNING

When I look back it seems as if the war did end that night.

Actually it went on for six months more, and we had a good deal of campaigning and some very hard fighting to do before the end came. But as far as Sheridan's men were concerned, the climax came that day at Cedar Creek. After that it was downhill all the way.

For a month after the battle we kept on the move, mopping up and trying to break the last of the guerilla bands that were such a dangerous nuisance. Sheridan sent the Sixth Corps back to Grant's army in front of Richmond, and most of the rest of the infantry was sent over into West Virginia. When winter came we were pretty largely a cavalry command once more.

It was cold and there was deep snow, and the snow was good. It hid the blackened, burned-out places, the fields that had been ravaged, the charred timbers of ruined barns and houses, and it made little white mounds over the hundreds and hundreds of graves that marked the places where the armies had been. The Valley began to look fresh and unstained and new again, as if all of the suffering and terror were over and people could make a fresh start and begin to live their own lives again when spring came.

It was a queer winter, in a way. We knew victory was near and the war would end before long. The boys were in high spirits, making jokes about the fighting they'd done and telling fancy tales about all of the great things they were going to do after the war. I felt the same way myself; when I thought that some day Lavinia might be back in Michigan with me, it seemed to me that I was the luckiest person alive. Yet under everything I had a sad, melancholy feeling.

When you were with Sheridan war could seem exciting, romantic, and even sort of gay. As long as I live, my pulse will beat faster when I remember that ride from Winchester to Cedar Creek, with a broken army pulling itself together again to the sound of fifteen miles of cheers; the sight of six thousand mounted men with drawn sabers charging across a plain in the flaming sunset to take a rank of Rebel guns; the breath-taking swing and stir of galloping along a battle line at Sheridan's stirrup as he waved his hat and drew the men forward. Those things were grand and I can never forget them.

But I can never forget, either, that war really isn't any of those things. They happened, and I can still see them happening, yet they are like the lying stories we used to tell the stay-at-homes after the war, just to make them envious of us. They happened but they are not the truth about war; and that winter I began to see that war is really something very different.

War is a tired courier, shot from his horse at the end of

ten hours in the saddle by guerillas who killed him to get his boots—not because they were trying to defend their country. It is a Virginia farmer hanged to a tree because some officer decided he might be a guerilla. It is the women who came to our headquarters that winter to beg bread and bacon from the army whose stragglers had robbed their homes of the food they needed to keep their children alive. It is the lost, hopeless look we saw in the eyes of men who stood by and watched while we burned their barns; or the hatred that stared at us from the faces of the women in the streets of the Valley towns.

Worst of all, it is the needless, useless, senseless cruelty and pain that go with a war, not doing any good to anybody, not helping to win the war, just happening because a war is going on, leaving you wondering if anything makes any sense.

Like what happened to Otis Cleverdun, for instance.

Otis had been off on some sort of scouting job, one day that winter, with a couple of other boys, and they came riding back to camp at the end of a gray, miserable sort of day, with a wet snow coming down and everything all muddy and dark. They were dressed like guerillas, and came up to one of our outposts in the twilight, shouting a password they'd been given to tell our pickets that they were Sheridan's men and not Rebels.

But there'd been a slip-up somewhere and the pickets at this post hadn't been told about the password. I think they hadn't been very alert, and apparently they came to all of a sudden, saw these riders coming up out of the gloom, and mistook them for some of Mosby's men.

Somebody yelled: "Guerillas!" Somebody else called

out: "Give it to the sons of guns!" and the pickets raised their carbines and let fly, firing as fast as they could pump the levers of their repeaters.

The scouts pulled up short, trying to call out that they belonged to Sheridan's team. Otis fell out of his saddle dead, with two bullets in his head, while another boy got a broken arm that the surgeons had to amputate . . . then the pickets realized their mistake and the firing stopped. Somebody called a surgeon and an ambulance, and that was that.

They laid Otis out back by the headquarters tents, and while a detail was digging a grave Joss and I went around to look at him. I stood staring down at him, remembering the kid who had thought up the stunt of writing "18" on a piece of paper and tucking it inside his shoe, the small-town kid who had turned into such a toughie and carried a guerilla's gold watch in his pocket. I said I hoped Sheridan would crack down hard on the stupid pickets who had made the mistake and killed one of our own boys.

Joss looked at me curiously.

"Why?" he asked. "What good would that do? This just happened, that's all. It's happened to these scouts before and it will again. That's one of the chances they take."

"But it's so useless!" I cried. "Otis got killed, and his death doesn't mean anything. It isn't as if he'd got killed in a battle. His life is just wasted."

"Well," said Joss, "that's war for you. You've known a lot of boys that got killed. What does any of it mean? It's just war, that's all."

It seemed to me that Joss was right, and maybe nothing made any sense. Under the flags and the bugles and the fine words, maybe this was what war really meant—a kid with half his head blown off, not because we'd had a fight but just because somebody had made a mistake. I had had all the war I ever wanted.

. . . In the spring we rode to the upper end of the Valley and destroyed the pitiful remnant of Early's army. Then we turned east through a gap in the Blue Ridge and rode down to join Grant's main army in front of Richmond and Petersburg, burning and destroying as we went. Sheridan was always at the head of the column, pulling us on. He said the Confederacy was dying on its feet and he wanted his cavalry to be in at the death, and finally we were.

Somewhere else, I suppose, you can read all about our last battles; how we broke the Confederate line at Five Forks, capturing six thousand prisoners and forcing Lee to retreat toward the south; how we chased his beaten army, never giving it a chance to rest, outrunning it and at last getting around in front of it and forcing it to a halt; how Sheridan led the way, a terrible swift sword striking where Grant wanted him to strike and at last cutting the life out of Lee's army and compelling it to surrender.

I went through it all. Sometimes I was excited, sometimes I was scared, and at the end I threw my cap in the air and cheered with everybody else. Yet, for me, it was as if the war had really been settled when the Sixth Corps went forward at Cedar Creek, as if everybody who died after that might just as well have lived.

The truth of it, I imagine, is that the war had not changed at all. It was just what it always had been, and it was I who had changed. I had grown older, I had grown tougher, I had learned a great many things I hadn't known before, and if I hadn't done anything else I had at least found out a few things about myself.

I would never run away from things again, leaving a faked note in a book, hiking fifteen miles in the dead of night, listening to see if I could hear relentless footsteps on the road behind me; and I wouldn't do any more aimless dreaming about the high adventure that lay somewhere beyond the horizon. I knew better now. I knew the only thing you really have to lick is something you carry with you: you can't run from it; sooner or later you have to face up to it; and if you do, then any place you happen to be, even if it's a tiny little town like Pine Bay, has boundless horizons. I knew that war is a preparation, not an end in itself, and that what it means to you will depend very largely on what you do after it has ended. . . .

Lee surrendered, and after a time Sheridan and his cavalry went back to Washington for a big review, with bands playing, flags in the streets, people cheering, and the President himself standing in front of the White House to take the salute. We went into camp, and at last word came down that the 2d Michigan Cavalry was to go back to Grand Rapids to be mustered out of service, which meant that I was to go, too. Sheridan himself was under orders to go to Texas, to command an army being assembled there in case we should have to fight the French in Mexico, and some of the boys thought it would be fun to go down there with him. But all I could think of was how much I wanted to get out of the army and go home.

When I went into the headquarters tent to get my papers endorsed, Sheridan looked up from his desk, threw down his pen, and pushed his chair back.

"Sergeant," he said, "forget about these papers. Come down to Texas with me. I'll still need somebody to carry my flag. And after a while, if you want, I can fix up an appointment to West Point for you. Then one of these days you'll be a cavalryman with shoulder straps. Probably you'll be a major general before you get through. Our job isn't nearly done. We've got a long road ahead of us yet."

He was grinning at me, partly joking but mostly serious, and I knew there had been a time when I would have jumped at what he was offering. But now I just shook my head and said:

"Sir, I'd like to, but I've got to get back home."

He scratched his chin and asked:

"Along with a little schoolma'am from Winchester?"

I got red in the face, and nodded.

"Well, I hope you get her," he said. "Good luck to you."

He stood up and stuck out his hand—that hard brown fist I'll always remember as gripping and swinging an old felt hat in the midst of the battle smoke. I shook hands, a sergeant shaking hands with a major general, and for just a moment I had a wild longing to forget everything and go with him. He had given war itself a meaning for me, I had ridden with him and looked death right in its mocking eyes, and because I had ridden with him I had learned how to live. But I was on a new road now, and to follow it I couldn't follow Phil Sheridan. I was on my own.

Then I was out of the tent, with my papers in my pocket. I was in a daze. I tried to think how much I owed to the general, yet all that was really in my mind was that I'd just have time for a quick trip to Winchester before heading west.

There was something unreal and almost dreamlike about going up the Valley again with everything peaceful —no guerillas, no cavalry patrols, no picket lines, nobody shooting at anybody. We had a few troops in Winchester but they weren't doing anything or bothering anybody, and I didn't even need a pass. I went straight to the Edwards house.

Lavinia was out when I got there but the doctor was in, and he seemed glad to see me. We sat down in rocking chairs on the front porch, and he wanted to know what I was going to do next. I told him how General Sheridan had asked me to stay in the army and go to Texas, but that I was going to get my discharge instead and go back home, and he nodded as if to say that I was doing the right thing.

"How do you feel, now that the war is ended?" he asked.

I looked down the quiet little street. Two women were standing by a fence, passing the time of day as if there was no hurry about anything. A couple of small boys were going along the walk, barefooted, talking like sixty about something or other, not noticing anybody or anything except their own little concerns. An old colored man was driving a mule hitched to a rickety buckboard, peddling blackberries, calling out his wares in a soft, quavery sort of chant that was like one of the regular early summer noises you hear without especially noticing. And all at once it seemed as if the war and all the terrible things that had happened in it were like some kind of dream that you look back on after you've waked up. It was daylight now; time to shake the dream off and get out of bed and get busy.

"Sir, I feel just fine," I told him.

He smiled, and said he was glad I felt that way. Then he said: "And here's Lavinia," and got up, smiled again, and limped into the house.

Lavinia came up the walk with a market basket on her arm. She had taken off a big broad-brimmed straw hat and was carrying it in the other hand. She saw me, and she was smiling as she came up the steps and I walked over to her —a funny little smile, as if she was surprised and a little uncertain.

"You *did* come back," she said.

I took her hand. I found that I had her basket in my other hand, although I couldn't remember having taken it from her. She tossed her hat in a chair and looked up at me, and for a minute neither of us seemed to have anything to say.

"Well," she said, "it's all over, isn't it?"

She meant the war, of course, but I felt that I had to correct her.

"No, it isn't over," I said. "It's just beginning. I'm going to get out of the army and go back to Michigan. As soon as I get things settled there I'm coming back and get you and then we're going out there together——"

I hadn't known I was going to blurt things out like that, and it surprised me as much as it surprised her. As a matter of fact, I believe it surprised me a good deal more than it surprised her. She had stopped smiling, and was looking at me very seriously, her eyes wide, her lips parted.

I remembered how she had teased me, and I hurried to add:

"Ma'am!"

Then she smiled, and I knew she was going to go with me.